PRAISE FOR CHRISTINA McDONALD

Praise for *What Lies In Darkness*

“Utterly compelling. In Detective Jess Lambert, McDonald has captured the perfect mix of gritty determination and haunted soul. With twists and turns everywhere, *What Lies in Darkness* delivers the kind of page-turner you don’t just read, but devour.”

—Lisa Gardner, New York Times bestselling author

"*What Lies In Darkness* is a smart, twisty thriller you won’t soon forget. Expertly crafted, with complex and fascinating characters. I am hooked on the Jess Lambert series, it keeps getting better and better.”

—Samantha Downing, internationally bestselling author

“Shocking, atmospheric, and tense, *What Lies In Darkness* is an emotionally powerful and twisty page-turner. With rich prose and multi-faceted characters, McDonald has expertly crafted a genre-bending supernatural thriller, making it an absolute must read!"

—Jeneva Rose, New York Times bestselling author

"What Lies In Darkness is a riveting story about the love of family, the devastation of loss, and the secrets we keep. And it has earned Christina McDonald a place in the pantheon of thriller-writer greats. Change your plans for the night because you won't be able to put this one down."

—Alex Finlay, critically-acclaimed author of *What Have We Done*

"With richly drawn characters and striking imagery, Christina McDonald delivers a taut, thick-with-atmosphere puzzler that doubles as a meditation on resilience in the face of trauma and an exploration of the sacrifices we make for those we love. Don't miss it!"

—E.G. Scott, international bestselling author of *The Rule of Three*

"Skilfully plotted with finely tuned prose, this compelling thriller will leave readers wanting more from McDonald and the flawed but wonderfully human protagonist she's created!"

—Wendy Walker, Nationally Bestselling Author of *What Remains*

"Jess Lambert is my new favorite detective! Christina McDonald's *What Lies In Darkness* is a must read. Every single character leaps off the page. The story grabbed me on page one and didn't let go until the last shocking, twisty page!"

—Debra Webb, USA Today bestselling author of *All The Little Truths*

"*What Lies in Darkness* is both a smart and edgy mystery and a searing portrayal of loss and betrayal. In Detective Jess Lambert, McDonald has gifted crime fiction with an unforgettable lead, a woman both in love with and struggling against the ghosts that haunt her. This is the perfect book for readers who love their thrillers fast-paced and deeply emotionally intelligent."

—Ashley Winstead, author of *Midnight is the Darkest Hour*

Praise for *These Still Black Waters*

"Atmospheric and inventive, Christina McDonald's *These Still Black Waters* pulled me in on page one and held tight. In this haunting and beautifully written thriller chock full of secrets that won't stay buried, McDonald is a masterful storyteller. A truly nightmarish trip to the lake guaranteed to keep readers enthralled."

—Heather Gudenkauf, New York Times bestselling author of *The Overnight Guest*

"*These Still Black Waters* has it all: electric writing, complex characters, a touch of the supernatural, and whiplash twists guaranteed to keep you up long past your bedtime."

—Jess Lourey, Amazon Charts bestselling author of *The Quarry Girls*

"Christina McDonald always delivers a gripping, twisty thriller, and *These Still Black Waters* is no exception. Detective Jess Lambert, damaged both physically and emotionally, must stop a killer set on avenging the dark secrets of the past. But as the body count rises, and the story hurtles toward a shocking and unique reveal, Jess must face her own demons before it's too late."

—Robyn Harding, bestselling author of *The Perfect Family*

"No one does dark heartbreak like Christina McDonald—and this captivating thriller wraps its sinister self around you the minute you begin. Gorgeously written and deeply immersive, this relatable story of envy and grief and motherhood and friendship will also haunt you long after you close the final shocking pages. Edgy, original, and completely surprising, *These Still Black Waters* is a triumph of storytelling."

—Hank Phillippi Ryan, USA Today bestselling author of *The House Guest*

"Christina McDonald shines in *These Still Black Waters*, a dark and dazzling thriller. The twists and turns culminate in an ending we promise you won't see coming. Highly recommend!"

—Liz Fenton and Lisa Steinke, authors of *Forever Hold Your Peace*

"A whip-smart and completely unexpected story of a killer out for revenge and a damaged detective out to stop him, a phenomenal story built on gorgeous prose and twists so surprising they'll leave you breathless. This is not the book you think it is, and I mean that in the best possible way."

—Kimberly Belle, internationally bestselling author of *The Personal Assistant*

Praise for *Do No Harm*

"Gripping and unflinching, *Do No Harm* explores the ferocity of a mother's love—and shows, in heartbreaking detail, how she'll risk everything to save her child."

—Sarah Pekkanen, New York Times bestselling author of *The Wife Between Us* and *You Are Not Alone*

"*Do No Harm* is a pulse-pounding deep dive into the dark heart of addiction. The stakes couldn't be higher in this smart, breathlessly paced, and emotional novel about love, family, and how far we'll go when our child's life hangs in the balance. Riveting, ripped from the headlines, and not to be missed."

—Lisa Unger, New York Times bestselling author of *Confessions on the 7:45*

"Christina McDonald has a real talent for bringing suburban domestic suspense to life and showcases it to great effect in *Do No Harm*. Tense, taut, and absolutely unmissable, you'll find yourself wondering how far YOU would go to save your child's life."

—J. T. Ellison, New York Times bestselling author of *Lie to Me*

"McDonald takes the heart-wrenching premise that has become her trademark and ratchets it up a notch in *Do No Harm*, blurring the lines between good and evil in a doctor desperate to save her sick child. A gripping, emotional roller coaster with a sting in the tail."

—Kimberly Belle, internationally bestselling author of *The Marriage Lie*

"Christina McDonald knows how to pack an emotional punch! *Do No Harm* is a riveting, thought-provoking novel that keeps you reading even as it breaks your heart. This might be my favorite book by McDonald yet."

—Samantha Downing, USA Today bestselling author of *My Lovely Wife*

"A gripping page-turner with a heart-wrenching moral quandary at its core. *Do No Harm* is tense, moving, and disturbingly relevant."

—Robyn Harding, internationally bestselling author of *The Swap* and *The Party*

"Devastating, heartbreaking, and incredibly timely—this risky and brilliant examination of when the ends justify the means will captivate you from moment one. The talented Christina McDonald dissects the crumbling marriage of two good people, and reveals how love and obsession can combine to destroy even the most perfect family. As a doctor's vow of 'do no harm' twists into 'do whatever it takes,' you'll be riveted by this thought-provoking and tragically believable story."

—Hank Phillippi Ryan, USA Today bestselling author of *The Murder List*

"With her trademark emotionally gripping, outstanding writing, Christina McDonald tackles the moral and ethical lines crossed by a doctor desperate to save her child. A stunning gut-punch of a suspense novel, *Do No Harm* expertly merges the dangers of the opioid crisis with a mother's love, leaving readers gasping for more. A breathtaking read."

—Samantha M. Bailey, #1 bestselling author of *Woman on the Edge*

"A gripping and unflinching novel. Christina McDonald demands an answer to the ultimate question: How far would you go to save your child? One thing is for sure: your heart will be ripped out as you whip through each page to discover the answer. Highly recommend!"

—Liz Fenton and Lisa Steinke, authors of *How to Save a Life*

"A family-driven medical thriller that's unique and propulsive, *Do No Harm* by Christina McDonald is as gut-wrenching as it is jaw-dropping. Not to be missed!"

—Hannah Mary McKinnon, bestselling author of *Sister Dear*

"Nobody writes motherhood like Christina McDonald. A riveting thriller that braids the complexities of modern parenting with the pressures of finding a moral center in a devastating opioid crisis. Heartrending, heart-pounding, and fearless to the last word."

—Amber Cowie, author of *Loss Lake*

Praise for *Behind Every Lie*

"*Behind Every Lie* is a deep, suspenseful novel packed with family secrets. Christina McDonald has a true gift for creating characters that are so well developed, it feels like you know them. An outstanding achievement!"

—Samantha Downing, author of the #1 international bestseller *My Lovely Wife*

"In *Behind Every Lie*, Christina McDonald brilliantly intertwines page-turning suspense with jaw-dropping family secrets. An emotionally charged domestic thriller that is sure to please!"

—Wendy Walker, national bestselling author of *The Night Before*

"A riveting collision of motherhood and memory—where a sinister and inescapable past haunts those struggling to make sense of their lives and protect their children. What's *Behind Every Lie* is a shocking truth—and for readers, a jaw-dropping, page-turning whirlwind of a thriller. Instantly captivating and endlessly surprising! Christina McDonald is a star."

—Hank Phillippi Ryan, USA Today bestselling author of *The Murder List*

"A clever, tense, and absorbing novel—this tale of family secrets had me racing toward the final pages."

—Emma Rous, bestselling author of *The Au Pair*

"Christina McDonald follows up her smashing debut *The Night Olivia Fell* with another winner. McDonald starts with a bang, then builds the action steadily, a gradual unfolding of secrets and lies that will have you constantly switching alliances. Read it like I did, in one sitting and straight through to the end, because you won't want to put this one down."

—Kimberly Belle, international bestselling author of *Dear Wife*

"Christina McDonald's *Behind Every Lie* is a layered, gut-wrenching domestic thriller that explores the complexities of mothers and daughters and the secrets families keep. Smart and intense, and with more than enough twists to give you whiplash, McDonald's beautiful, emotional storytelling will leave you breathless. I don't think I exhaled until the end."

—Jennifer Hillier, author of *Jar of Hearts*, ITW Award winner for Best Novel

"Christina McDonald's *Behind Every Lie* is a cleverly plotted and emotionally charged page-turner about memory, trusting yourself, grieving, and letting go. Family secrets run deep in this compelling exploration of how far a mother will go to protect her child. Full of twists and turns, this is domestic suspense at its best!"

—Karen Katchur, bestselling author of *River Bodies*

"In *Behind Every Lie*, a lightning-strike survivor discovers that memories are fallible, identities are fungible, and she can't trust anyone—including herself. With nuanced and dubiously trustworthy characters, dual timelines revealing decades of secrets, and a tension-packed plot, Christina McDonald has crafted an engrossing and utterly addictive thriller. I couldn't turn the pages fast enough!"

—Kathleen Barber, author of *Truth Be Told*

"Addictive and emotionally resonant, *Behind Every Lie* is a twisty, fast-paced thriller with secrets nestled inside secrets. Nothing is as it seems in this story exploring the sorrow and strength of brokenness, and with complex characters and a relentlessly compelling plot, you'll be unable to stop reading it—or forget it once you do."

—Megan Collins, author of *The Winter Sister*

Praise for *The Night Olivia Fell*

"The *Night Olivia Fell* by Christina McDonald is a stunning thriller that instantly grabbed me by the throat and wouldn't let go until the final, poignant sentence. McDonald artfully brings to the page the emotionally fraught, complex relationship between mother and daughter in this atmospheric, absorbing page-turner. *The Night Olivia Fell* cracked my heart into a million pieces and then slowly pieced it back together again."

—Heather Gudenkauf, New York Times bestselling author of *The Weight of Silence* and *Not a Sound*

"In Christina McDonald's *The Night Olivia Fell*, Abi gets the call every mother fears: her daughter has fallen from a bridge and is brain-dead . . . but was it an accident or a crime? McDonald reveals the answer in steady, page-turning increments, a gradual unfolding of truths and long-held secrets that culminates in a heart-wrenching resolution. A suspenseful debut that packs an emotional punch."

—Kimberly Belle, international bestselling author of *Three Days Missing* and *The Marriage Lie*

"I was absolutely hooked; it was such an emotional read that I was broken by the end. Heartbreaking and thrilling at the same time."

—Jenny Blackhurst, bestselling author of *How I Lost You*

"Beautifully written and moving, with characters I felt I knew, *The Night Olivia Fell* is a stunning debut that kept me guessing right until the final, heartbreaking twist."

—Claire Douglas, bestselling author of *The Sisters*, *Local Girl Missing*, and *Last Seen Alive*

"Christina McDonald's *The Night Olivia Fell* takes a mother's worst nightmare to a whole new level. This is an intense, twisting, heartbreaking thriller that explores in painful detail the consequences of family secrets. The reader will be riveted until the final page . . . and may even feel a bit of hope when all is said and done. Don't miss this one!"

—David Bell, bestselling author of *Somebody's Daughter*

"Christina McDonald has crafted an emotionally charged mystery that will leave readers equally gut-wrenched and gripped. *The Night Olivia Fell* welcomes a talented new addition to the world of domestic suspense."

—Mary Kubica, New York Times bestselling author of *The Good Girl* and *When the Lights Go Out*

The Stranger At Black Lake

Christina McDonald

OTHER TITLES BY CHRISTINA McDONALD

Jess Lambert Thrillers

What Lies In Darkness

These Still Black Waters

Other Titles

Do No Harm

Behind Every Lie

The Night Olivia Fell

The Stranger At Black Lake

A Jess Lambert Novella

CHRISTINA MCDONALD

Book Cover by Anna Dorfman

For my readers, who loved Jess Lambert
so much that I kept imagining.

Chapter 1

Jess

The text comes through early, as the birds are beginning to chirp and the lemony springtime sunshine is edging through the new blinds Mac just hung in our bedroom. There's only so long you can live in a new house without blinds.

He's out.

I know who "he" is, and my heart thumps, a squirt of fear.

I'm sorry, I was only just told. I'll find out more. Call me later.

"Who is it?" Mac murmurs.

"Just Leah wishing us good luck with the move," I lie.

I slip out of bed and push past half-empty moving boxes into the bathroom. I splash water on my face, brush my teeth, get changed for my morning run. When I finish, Mac is already dressed, tying a double Windsor in his tie.

I slide my arms around him and his lips drop to mine.

"Mmm, minty fresh," he says.

"Mmm, dog vomit breath." We've reached the stage in our marriage where we can joke about it rather than hiding it.

"Well, someone was hogging the bathroom."

"We have two now!" I swat his butt playfully. "I'm going for a run. Don't be late, you might get fired."

He laughs. He won't get fired. His dad owns the law firm.

I slip my running jacket on, zip my phone into the pocket, and turn to leave.

"Hey." Mac stops me. "You sure you'll be okay?"

Mac's hands are still working the tie, but I can see his fair brows are crumpled, his shoulders set in that way I know. I cross to him, take over tying the Windsor. The indigo brings out the warmth in his blue eyes.

My husband is a handsome man. I'm biased, obviously, but objectively, he is. He's classically good looking with high cheekbones and a straight nose, slim and tall with well-developed shoulders from years of rowing and swimming.

"Don't worry about me," I say. "Black Lake is a fresh start, and that's exactly what I need." I loop the wide end of the tie under and pull it tight. "I'm happy to be here."

I come from a military family. I'm used to moving. By the time we settled in New York after my dad switched from the Marines to the police, making and shedding friends was as easy for me as changing clothes. I can start over here. I've done it before.

I kiss Mac goodbye and slip out the door. Outside, spring has arrived in a hurry. The streets are bursting with cherry blossoms, bustling with people walking their dogs; parents walking their kids to school; couples saying goodbye, getting in their cars, heading to work.

I jog toward the lake, but after I turn the first corner, I drop into a walk and head to Black Lake's little market.

I'm not sure why I haven't told Mac I don't actually go for a run anymore. I did run when we first arrived a few weeks ago. But I quickly got bored of it. And then one day I stopped for a coffee. Then the next day, and the next.

I guess I just don't want to admit the truth to Mac: that I feel lonely, lost. I can't tell him I miss my job as a paramedic, the busy-ness of it, the fullness of each day. I miss our cramped apartment in Brooklyn. I miss the friends we left. I can't tell him I don't know who I am or where I belong.

What makes it even worse is that I'm not even sure I *want* to go back to being a paramedic. Maybe I should just find a new career. But what?

I glance at the faded scar on my forearm, a parting gift from a man who'd attacked me with a knife. I lost my confidence after that call.

But that's not all I lost.

Mac doesn't need to be distracted by my issues, and he definitely doesn't need to worry about the man who's been released from prison, who swore he'd find me when he got out.

I wind through the cobbled lanes to Black Lake's market, debating whether I'll call Leah back. I decide to wait until later, after my coffee.

The vendors are setting up, the air fresh with the scent of flowers being unloaded, freshly baked pastries being set out, coffee being brewed. I stop at the last stall and order a cappuccino and a croissant. The guy behind the counter is tall and beanpole thin, with gelled black hair and metal in his nose and ears. His name is Carl.

"Morning, Jess," Carl says. He makes the best cappuccino I've ever tasted. Or maybe I'm just more in tune to it these days, like my sense of taste has sharpened since I'm not constantly in fight or flight mode. "That'll be $4.25, please."

A chuckle comes from behind me. A woman with long, chestnut hair is grinning at me, seafoam green eyes sparkling. She is beautiful, with one of those exquisite faces you see in old movies, radiant creamy skin and full lips, a delicate, elfin chin. Her makeup is heavy, but artfully done. To look older or younger, I'm not quite sure. She's wearing a white linen wrap dress with gold jewelry at her wrists and ears, a wide-brimmed straw hat perched on her head.

"That's my lucky number."

She has a slight accent, something I can't quite place.

"Sorry?"

"The total for your order: $4.25. It's my birthday and I'm twenty-five. Twenty-five on the twenty-fifth."

"Today's your birthday?"

She smiles. "Yes. 4/25."

Her smile is so warm, I can't help but return it. "Well, happy birthday. Here, your order's on me."

"No, I couldn't..."

"I insist."

"Okay, well, thanks." She orders the same thing as me, then turns and sticks out a hand. "I'm Annie. Annie Jones."

"I'm Jess. My husband and I just moved to Black Lake."

Her eyes widen. "Me too! From Paraguay!"

"New York. God, it's hard, right? Trying to buy a new house, find out where the grocery store is, find a new job. I've never been without a job in my life."

"Ha! Same! I feel a little lost, to be honest."

"I know *exactly* what you mean." I smile. It's nice to feel understood.

We grab our lattes and walk along the lakefront trail, sitting on a bench that overlooks a wooden dock stretching into the lake. The surface of the water is black, glistening like oil in the morning sun. It is pretty here. Strips of golden sand fringe the lake as far as the eye can see, wooded islands dotting the surface. But there's something about the lake—those dark, bottomless waters; a nameless, inexplicable dread; a strange smell coming off it, like splintered branches and torn leaves and raw grief.

"We bought that house back there." Annie brings my attention back, waving over her shoulder at a ramshackle Victorian with leaded windows and small pink roses set back from the road and up the hill a little way. It's lovely, but unloved, unkempt. Dark shadows lurk in thick bramble and overgrown bushes.

"You live *there*?" I ask, surprised.

She gives a small laugh. "You've heard the rumors then?"

"I mean...yeah, I guess so. People say it's haunted. Mac, my husband, he grew up here. They called it the gingerbread house when he was a kid, and boy, he's told me some tales."

She leans closer, eyes glowing. "I heard the woman who lived there drowned herself in the lake. Just filled her pockets with rocks and walked right into the water to escape an unhappy marriage. After, she haunted her husband, a vengeful ghost who slowly drove him insane, until he finally killed himself. Now people say they see the ghost of a dripping wet woman walking between the house and the lake across the street."

"That's a terrible story!" I say, but Annie's laughing, and so am I, and I'm glad that at least she knows the stories about that house, otherwise finding out now would really actually suck. "I'm sure it's an old wives' tale."

"Yes. That's why we were willing to buy it. So, what brings you to Black Lake?" Annie asks.

I hesitate, then tell her a sanitized version of the truth. "Mac's dad finally convinced him to take up a position at his law firm. And the timing seemed right. I was a paramedic in New York, and the job was getting a little...intense... so I decided to take some time off."

"A paramedic! Gosh, you're like a real-life superhero."

"I don't know about that," I say with a laugh. "What about you? What brought you here?"

"Same. My husband." She settles her coffee on the bench and takes the lid off, tears open a packet of sugar, and dumps it into the cup. But her hands are shaking just slightly. Nervous? Or maybe detoxing. I've seen it before with my dad.

"Olly's a doctor at the hospital. I'm a teacher. I'll be starting at the elementary school in September."

A gentle breeze ruffles the brim of her straw hat. She reaches up, tucks her hair behind her ears. Her sleeves pull up and I think I see a ropy white scar on the underside of her wrists.

She drops her arms and steers the conversation back to me, what it was like being a paramedic, what it was like living in New York. We talk for nearly an hour, barely noticing the time passing.

Finally, Annie stands and says she needs to go. "I hope you won't think I'm too forward, but would you like to grab a drink sometime? My treat. It'll be my turn, you know, after the coffee."

"I would love that."

We exchange phone numbers and I wish her a happy birthday.

Before she leaves, she turns to me one last time. "Thank you, Jess. I don't believe in fate, but I think I'm lucky I met you today."

I smile. I hope she's right. "Thanks, Annie. I feel the same."

***

I go for a run after all. The thought of going back to our silent house, with nothing to do, makes my stomach clench.

I jog back through town, down a quaint, cobbled street, passing a cathedral, a library, an ice cream shop. Like most market towns, Black Lake is charming, if a little old fashioned. There's a cute gazebo in the park and lots of pretty riverside walks and forest hikes. It's everything Mac and I had been talking about: a quieter, more peaceful life. The type of small town that's good for raising a family.

I jog longer than I thought I would and when I next check my watch, over an hour has passed. I've looped around, taking the long way home through the forest and ending up back where I started at the lakefront.

I'm jogging along the sandy shore, just approaching the gingerbread house, when I see something. It's white and formless, twisting in the trees along the lake in front of me. It floats, light and flowing in the morning heat. I stop short, remembering Annie's story.

People say they see the wife wandering the lake, that both she and the husband haunt the house, warring ghosts competing for space.

I blink and the white thing disappears, replaced by something real, a woman with long, dark hair, stumbling across the road toward the water. I recognize her instantly.

Annie.

I start to call her name, then stop short.

Because besides a pair of red canvas shoes, she is completely and totally bare-ass naked.

My mind jumps to the scar on the inside of her wrist, the shaking hands. A psychotic break, perhaps? I go into paramedic mode, even as I acknowledge that I should call 911. I'm not mentally or physically equipped to deal with this anymore.

But Annie doesn't seem like she's hallucinating or having delusions. If anything, she seems completely, chillingly still. She looks like she needs help.

So I go to her.

"Annie!" She doesn't appear to hear me.

I pick up my pace and call out again. "Annie, wait!"

She turns, her hair swinging over one shoulder, exposing a tattoo inked across the top half of her back. It's a snake eating its own tail, and inside the circle of the snake's body are words I don't recognize: Memento Mori.

"I...do you know you're naked?" I ask stupidly.

Annie's green eyes are glazed. Shock? I run my eyes over her, making a quick assessment, as I'm trained to do. She doesn't appear to be on drugs; there's no smell of alcohol on her.

"Are you okay?"

No answer.

"Here." I shed my thin running jacket and offer it to her.

Her hands, small and fine, are slack against her pale, naked thighs. Finally, she lifts them, raising both arms like a child waiting to be dressed. I wrap the coat under her arms like a towel, so it covers her boobs and half her butt.

"Shall I take you to your house?" I ask gently.

She turns and crosses the road, heading back up the slight embankment to the gingerbread house. I follow her bright red shoes like a beacon. But there's something about them, those shoes...

She's already opening a rusted little metal gate with tiny pink roses twisted and twined around an arched trellis. The hinges groan, setting my teeth on edge as I catch up to her.

"Did you leave the front door open?" I ask.

Annie doesn't answer. She just stands there, her hands loose at her sides, her red shoes bright against her pale, slender legs. She's shivering, I realize.

I glance again at the door. It's intact. No sign of forced entry here. But still, a bad feeling shivers somewhere deep inside my spine, like a sound too low to hear, a warning, a threat, a premonition.

I hesitate, but when I look at Annie, I see she's shaking, fear and shock frozen on her face.

"Let's get you inside," I say gently.

I push the door open wider and step into the house.

Red.

There's so much red. Everywhere. Smeared across the hardwood floors in the living room and over the beige couches. Trailing up the banister and the wooden stairs, streaked across the walls. Glistening, fresh, metallic. The rich, ripe scent of flayed meat is overwhelming.

I slowly turn to face Annie. That's when I realize.

Annie's shoes aren't red. They're soaked in blood.

Chapter 2

Him

Silence.

You wouldn't think it would be so loud. But it is.

Inside, there is never silence. Never a moment to be by yourself, to think. It is the noise that got me most inside. Even in the dead of night, there is always sound from somewhere. There's the hum of the lights, the shouts of the inmates, the perpetual, constant movement of other men moving, farting, fighting, fucking, groaning, screaming, shouting. But never silence.

I suppose it isn't silence, exactly, out here. The occasional rustle of a rat, the call of a fox, the hoot of an owl. The wind tickling the pine trees or the clicking of bats as they dive into the night. It isn't pure silence, but it's peaceful all the same.

I lower myself onto the grass and lie down, letting my fingers travel across it. It is cool, just shy of damp, and soft, like a feather caressing my hand. There was nothing soft inside, either. Just scratchy pillows and a lumpy mattress, the occasional hard fist or shove into the wall. Even the sounds were hard, sharp-edged shrieks and guttural roars.

This is my bed tonight, this carpet of grass surrounded by the arching pine trees.

I am free. Finally, after nearly twenty years of being in prison, free. And no matter what happens this time, I'm not going back.

Don't let your past own you, Nic, the prison counselor had told me before they released me. *Wherever there's ignorance, there's stigma, but you can be anything you want to be. Leave your past in the past.*

Total bullshit, if you ask me. Your past is a part of you. You can't leave it behind. It's the bad angel on your shoulder, waiting to bite you in the head.

I laugh, a sharp sound that sends a squirrel or raccoon rustling in the bushes. I'm not scared of them. They're less likely to hurt me than the men inside were, and even they mostly stayed away. Once, when I was first inside, I got my ass kicked by a tall, built-like-a-tank Nazi. He'd burst one of the lumps on my body and white puss and red blood squirted out, covering him. After that, word spread. Nobody wanted to touch me, which wasn't the worst thing. They didn't even want to look at me. When they did, I could see the revulsion in their eyes, the disgust bordering on horror.

I get it. With over a thousand tumors all over my body, I'm a monster. I started developing the benign lumps under my skin when I was a teenager. They're noncancerous, but completely debilitating. In more ways than one.

With a diagnosis–neurofibromatosis–came scoliosis, crippling headaches, surgeries, pain. Before I dropped out of high school, someone started calling me Mr. Bump, like I was a gruesome Mr. Men character, and the name stuck.

I got looks of revulsion wherever I went. A child tugging on his mother's hand in fear; secret, horrified looks from women at the grocery store. The disgust from other prisoners when I stripped for a shower.

She had that look, the last time I saw her. Like she couldn't recognize what I'd become.

You have to control whatever's inside of you, I remember her saying. *Control yourself or they win.*

I was never very good at controlling anything. I always struggled to express what I was thinking, eventually getting another dirty diagnosis, ADHD. Words were tough. I was better with my hands and fists.

Under the twinkling stars, I pull a small compact mirror from the back of my sweats pocket, the same sweats I was wearing when I first went in, and gently peel the balaclava from my head. I awkwardly make my way into a slip of moonlight streaming between the pines and hold the mirror up. I do this daily; have always done this daily.

Ever since I was diagnosed, I'd wake in the morning and make the painful journey to the full-length bathroom mirror. Peering into the glass, I'd anxiously check my body from head to toe, terrified that more lumps had appeared overnight.

The man looking back at me is worse than the kid who was diagnosed all those years ago. Nothing has changed. I am still a monster. A monster with a new lump growing on the side of his nose. One to add to the hundreds of others on my face.

I scratch the fleshy tumor. It bulges and dips, squishy and thick, like a bag of worms squirming under the pressure of my finger. I press harder. The pain is a siren in my head, growing and growing until it's blaring. *Alert, alert, alert!*

Stop it, Nic. I can hear her voice inside my head. *Put the knife down. You don't want to do that.*

I'm a monster.

You're not a monster, you're a superhero.

I lie back on the grass once more, still staring at myself, the gnarled tumors and uneven, gray-washed skin, pocked-marked with scars. My age is hiding in the lines scored around my eyes, the shadows stark beneath them.

Tomorrow I'll hop a cargo train heading the direction I need to go. Before I left, I used the prison library computer to look up the timetable. But for now, sleep.

I snap the compact shut and, with great difficulty, slide it back into my sweats. I stretch out, unfolding my body on the soft grass, letting my arms and legs spread out, listening to the sounds of the darkness, the night drifting by, wind gently ruffling the pine trees.

In the darkness, her face forms in my head, and I feel a sudden, overwhelming surge of emotion clogging my throat with tears and bitterness. I hear her voice, even in these moments just before I drift off to sleep, her words echoing through my head, filling in my dreams with color and light and life.

"You're a superhero," I whisper to myself.

I'm far away from her now, far away from that place, from the bars that trapped me for too long.

But I'm free. And tomorrow, even though she doesn't know it yet, I'm coming for her.

Chapter 3

Jess

I'm frozen, acutely aware of the butchery in front of me and the woman behind me. There's not enough light. Not enough air. Something primal is buzzing inside me, urging me to get the hell out of here. I ignore it and step deeper into the house.

The walls are half-paneled, dark wood at the bottom, peeling, dusty, off-white wallpaper at the top. The blood is mostly concentrated here, in the living room. It has pooled, slick and wet, in the middle of the dark, scarred hardwood floor. Streaks of it are splattered across the wallpaper. Dark crimson is splashed over the couches like a serial killer's painting.

I turn in a full circle, pressing a hand to my mouth as I try not to gag. I lift my eyes to an antique-looking table that sits flush against the living room wall. A glass case sits in the middle, and inside is a two-pronged stand holding some sort of...necklace? The wall above it is smeared with blood. No, not smeared. *Scrawled.* Somebody has written in big letters across the wall:

Memento Mori.

A chill skitters down my spine. The same words that are tattooed on Annie's back.

I turn to Annie, my racing heart pulsing so fast I almost feel dizzy. But she still looks like she's in shock, her eyes wide, face blank.

I step closer to the red, glistening wall like a woman hypnotized, cast under some sort of evil spell.

The necklace under the blood-scrawled words: Memento Mori. It's propped up on a stand inside the glass case. But once I get closer I see that it isn't a necklace at all. It looks like a rosary delicately carved from some sort of honey-hued material. Ivory. Or maybe bone. The rosary features a series of small beads that, on closer inspection, are delicately carved skulls, their eyes dark holes that somehow seem like they're staring right at me. The largest, final bead is three-sided, featuring a man, a woman, and a skull.

I tear my eyes from the sight and turn in a slow circle. On a wooden coffee table is a recyclable cup, the logo of the café where I bought Annie a coffee this morning clearly visible. On the floor next to the pool of blood is the wide-brimmed straw hat that Annie was wearing earlier, now streaked with blood. And next to the door, folded neatly, is her white linen dress.

Somebody has been violently attacked here. There's no way they could've lived with this amount of blood loss.

Except...

Where is the body?

Behind Annie, a sliding glass door leads to an untended back yard. A cracked and broken gate hangs half-off its hinges at the perimeter. A hummingbird flits around a blossoming Granny Smith apple tree, oblivious to the carnage inside. I recognize the clusters of pinkish-white flowers from my own backyard.

The sliding door is closed. I try the handle. Locked. No sign of forced entry.

From this vantage point, I notice a trail of blood leading deeper into the house. I follow it, stepping over bloody patches, careful not to disturb any evidence. A doorway opens to a long, rectangular kitchen that overlooks a dense tangle of trees and bushes and a small patio cracked and overtaken by weeds.

A part of me knows I should get the hell out of here, call the cops, get someone else to deal with this. But another part of me–the paramedic who's spent her entire adult life responding to emergencies–is telling me to find whoever's hurt. Get them help. If it isn't too late.

But it is too late. I realize that as soon as I step inside the kitchen.

The body lies prone in the middle of the white-tiled floor. It's so white. Bright white. Like an ad for a cleaning product. Or maybe that's just because of the stark contrast of blood against the white tiles, splashed onto the modern, white and stainless steel cupboards.

Blood is seeping from the man's head, his neck, his chest. There are dozens of stab wounds all over his body. His eyes are open, unseeing. His jeans are blood-soaked, his loose linen shirt saturated as well. He wears socks that must have been white once, but are now bright red.

The faint sound of buzzing has already started, fat flies excited by the scent of death. I try to breathe through my mouth as I survey the scene. Bloody handprints mark the floor, along with long streaks of blood. It looks like he tried to drag himself in here. Or someone did it for him.

A set of bloody footprints move in a circle around the body, then to a door on the far side of the kitchen. It's partially open, maybe leading to a basement, or a cellar. The door, I notice, locks from the outside.

Why would anybody have a basement door that locks from the outside?

I turn in a circle, my eyes settling again on the man, Annie's poor murdered husband. I've seen dead bodies before. Young mothers who've OD'd on oxy. Fathers shot in gang drive-bys. Children killed in hit-and-runs. But this. This is anger. *Fury*. This man has been stabbed a couple of dozen times.

It's clear just from a glance that he's dead, but I check anyway, thrusting my fingers to his neck, feeling for his carotid artery, which, amazingly, is the only place he hasn't been stabbed. He didn't die quickly, that's for sure.

There's no pulse.

I hear a sound and whirl, heart pounding.

"Annie." She's come up behind me, hovering in the shadows of the kitchen doorway. She's still wearing my jacket wrapped around her middle.

I swallow hard, my throat now dry and sticky. "Who did this?"

And then a thought, lightning fast: was it you?

Annie doesn't answer, but she's shivering harder than ever. She looks up, her eyes scanning the house, as if seeing it for the first time. Her face is calm, almost numb. Like she's completely disassociated from what's happened here. And yet, there's something about her eyes, something...alert.

"I have to call the police," I tell her.

Still, no answer.

I watch her warily. Even if she's in shock, she could snap out of it any moment. I've let my guard down before. That's how it happened last time, the man with the knife.

Keeping my back to the wall, my front facing her, I pull my phone from my running belt and dial 911. I tell the dispatcher where we are, what the scene is like, that the victim is definitely dead. I assure her that Annie is still at the scene, that she appears uninjured but is in shock.

"Send an ambulance," I tell the dispatcher. "She needs help."

I hang up and turn to Annie. "The ambulance and police will be here shortly. They'll take care of you, okay? You don't have to worry. You're safe."

I glance again at the dead man. "Can you tell me what happened, Annie? Who did this?"

She still doesn't say anything, but her teeth are clattering together, goosebumps prickling her pale, white flesh.

I know from experience that when the police arrive she will be checked over, then taken to a hospital, possibly a police station. She'll be interrogated, examined. Compassion swells in me.

"I'll get you some clothes," I say. "Is your bedroom upstairs?"

Annie doesn't answer, so I guide her back out to the living room, where a patch of sun is streaming through the large sash windows, and tell her to wait, that I'll find her some clothes.

I run upstairs, careful not to step in the bloody footprints. The stairs are carpeted, an old-fashioned sort of shag carpeting that was maybe green once upon a time, but now looks gray. By the time I reach the top of the stairs, the footsteps have disappeared, as if the blood on the killer's shoes had been wiped dry. Or they'd taken their shoes off. Could the killer still be here? My heart thumps and I freeze, listening.

I don't hear anything, so I inch forward, throwing doors open as I go. There are three bedrooms on this floor, again with lots of wood paneling, wood flooring, dusty, old-fashioned wallpaper. Everything is sparsely furnished, half-full boxes in each room, as if somebody hasn't quite finished unpacking.

The master bedroom overlooks the lake. There's a king-size bed covered in a threadbare, navy blue duvet. On one bedside table is a lamp, a bottle of water, a phone charger, a silver-framed photo of the man I saw downstairs, an elderly couple–his parents?–and a petite blonde woman, impeccably coiffed with delicate features. His sister?

There is no clutter, no dirty clothes tossed on the floor, no shoes kicked into a corner, no pictures hanging on the walls. It all feels slightly impersonal. I suppose they've just moved here, perhaps that's it.

I hurry past the bed to a wood-paneled, walk-in closet. It appears to be a his and hers closet: his on the right, hers on the left. I yank a long-sleeve t-shirt from a hanger and turn to the dresser by the bed, rummaging through the drawers. I pull out soft jersey jogging bottoms, underwear, a bra. At the bottom of the underwear drawer, my hands smack against something. I feel blindly in the drawer, grasp the item, and pull out a gun.

I drop it like I've been burned and curse. Now I'll have to explain to the police that I came upstairs, that my fingerprints might be on the gun. I carefully settle it back in place, cover it, leaving it like I found it. My fingers knock against something else. Something lying amid the frilly lace panties and underwear. Not buried, like the gun, but set on top of the clothing. An old, faded picture in a small, metal frame. In it are two boys, adolescents, and a girl perhaps a year or two older. Annie and her brothers?

Something flickers in my peripheral vision, a flash of white. I whirl, stare out into the hallway, my heart hammering. Just a trick of the light, maybe.

I drop the picture back into the drawer and turn to leave. I don't know if Annie is the victim or perpetrator, but I know I can't let her leave, so I'm anxious to get back down to her. But then I notice something sitting on top of the dresser. It looks like a copy of a newspaper article.

The Black Lake Echo, March 21, 1996

Police are appealing for information regarding two teenagers who have been missing since the violent death of their father, Jacob Haynes, at Lakeside Road on Sunday night. J.J. and Alan Haynes are not thought to be involved, but police are concerned as they've been missing since Mr. Haynes's body was found, along with a note confirming he'd taken his own life. Police are keen to speak to them and are concerned for their safety.

"We want to make sure J.J. and Alan are okay and haven't come to any harm," Detective Tony Morretti of the Black Lake Police Department told the press.

Alan is fifteen and is described as having longish brown hair and brown eyes. He was last seen wearing a Seinfeld t-shirt and jeans with white tennis shoes. J.J. (Jacob Jr.) is twelve, small for his age, with a café au lait mark on his left cheek. He has sandy blond hair and brown eyes and was last seen wearing white tennis shoes, light jeans, and a gray ho odie.

Anyone with any information about the whereabouts of the teenagers, or who might have seen them, should contact Black Lake Police urgently.

Lakeside Road. That's here. The gingerbread house. The man in this article committed suicide here in this very house. And now another man's been murdered.

I drop the article back onto the dresser and hurry down the stairs, clothes clutched in my hands.

"Here, Annie," I call to her. "You'll want to get dressed before they get here."

I look around at the blood-splattered living room.

But Annie is no longer there.

Chapter 4

Jess

I'm waiting outside the house when the police arrive. An ambulance pulls up next, followed by an unmarked police car: a detective.

The detective introduces himself as Luis Rivero. He is stout with a broad face and intense, dark eyes. Stubble shadows his jaw and his hair sticks up in little pieces, like brushwood in a forest. He was in the military before becoming a detective, has a *Semper Fidelis* tattoo on his left bicep. *Always Faithful* is the motto for the U.S. Marine Corps. I know because my dad has the same tattoo.

He wears dark slacks and a white button-down shirt, open at the collar, no jacket. He's calm with a still watchfulness that reminds me of my dad. His expression is inscrutable as he speaks, asking me clear questions that seek out the facts, nothing else.

I can tell he is annoyed that Annie has gone missing, but he doesn't say it out loud. "We've put out an APB for her with the description you've given us."

"I mean, she's naked. She can't be that hard to find," I say. "Someone will see her."

"Unless she had clothes stashed somewhere. A wig. A disguise. You never know with some people."

I hadn't thought of that and want to slink away in shame. Had she been playing me all along? Meeting me, chatting with me over coffee, leading me right to a crime scene? The proverbial scorpion riding my back all the way across the river.

But why?

I tell him about my morning, about meeting Annie Jones at the market, how she'd said she'd moved here from Paraguay. We'd chatted for an hour and exchanged numbers before she left and I went for a run. After my run, I saw her by the lake. Naked.

"So you don't really know Annie Jones? Who she is? Where she's from?" he asks.

"No...I...wait. Her coffee cup." I turn and point at the house. "It's in there on the coffee table. And, um, her straw hat. Oh, and her dress! It was white linen. Folded. By the front door. Maybe you could get DNA?"

"Wait here."

Detective Rivero hurries back into the house. He returns a few minutes later, shaking his head. "Nothing there. No coffee cup, no hat, no dress."

I frown. "She must've taken it. But...?"

I don't finish my sentence. Maybe she didn't want anybody to know who she really is. But why make plans with me? Why give me her phone number?

I tell the detective as much.

"Wait." He holds up a hand. "You have her phone number?"

I nod.

"Can we call it?"

I take my phone out and that's when I notice: I have a missed call. I show the detective.

"I missed a call from her at 10:42 a.m. I must've been running."

Guilt floods in. Maybe she needed my help. Maybe if I'd answered, I could've stopped this.

I dial Annie's number, but it goes directly to voicemail. Detective Rivero jots the number in his notebook and tells me he'll follow up on it.

"She appeared to be in shock, and when we approached the house, she became increasingly agitated. Fearful," I say.

Rivero's jaw tightens.

"Besides the bloody shoes, she was completely naked. I went to get her some clothes from upstairs. I'm so sorry, I shouldn't have left her."

Rivero shakes his head. "Not your fault."

"When I was upstairs, I saw a newspaper article just sitting on top of the dresser. It's still there. Do you think it has anything to do with what's happened?"

"It's too early to say, but I'll definitely look into it. Now, can you walk me through what happened?"

I tell him about the tattoo on Annie's back, the blood-soaked shoes, finding the body inside the house, as well as the gun in the underwear drawer, how it will have my prints on it. I walk through the scene in detail, from the lack of paintings on the walls to the memento mori scrawled above the glass-encased rosary to the type of blood splatter and the position of the body in the kitchen.

"Based on the blood trail from the living room into the kitchen, it looks like he was going for the phone," I say. "There was a cordless phone next to the toaster. But he bled out before he could get there."

Detective Rivero's brows lift. "I'm impressed. Your spatial memory is incredible."

He rolls up on the balls of his feet, then back. He's thinking hard about something.

"Why did you go inside?" he asks. "Why not call for help?"

"Initially, I could see the door hadn't been disturbed. There was no damage, no sign of breaking and entering. So I didn't think there was any danger. And given Annie's state, I thought perhaps she was ill and needed help. Once I got inside and saw the blood..." I shrug. "I'm a paramedic. I'm trained to help people."

He squints, looks closer at me. "You're a paramedic?"

I blush. "Not anymore. Not here in Black Lake, anyway. My husband and I have just moved here from New York. He grew up here. Malcolm Lambert. Mac?"

Rivero shakes his head, not recognizing Mac's name. Someone shouts from the house and he turns. I've already given him my contact details, so he hands me a business card and tells me he'll be in touch to get an official statement down at the police station soon, then ducks under the rose trellis and heads toward the house.

I shiver as I watch him walk away, glad I'm outside, away from the blood, the cloying scent of iron, the dark presence that seemed to lurk inside those wood-paneled walls.

For a moment I don't move. I hear Rivero talking to the uniformed cop about the body inside and I'm not ashamed to admit I move closer to eavesdrop a little.

"His wife's on the way," the cop says. "She'll be here soon. Get your game face on."

My breath catches in my throat.

The man inside the house isn't Annie's husband.

Then who the hell is he?

***

As soon as I get home, I shower, then change into jeans and a t-shirt. Downstairs, I make myself a roast beef sandwich with extra mayo and extra cheese, and pull out an old half-filled notebook from one of the boxes that still hasn't been unpacked in our spare bedroom. I find a pen in a drawer and begin making a list of all the things I know.

When I met her earlier, Annie Jones had said she was a teacher. Her husband was called Olly, and he was a doctor at the hospital. She said she lived in the gingerbread house; that they'd just moved there. Had it all been a lie?

I sketch the tattoo I saw on Annie's back of the snake eating its own tail, the words *memento mori* scrawled inside it. I'm not great at drawing, but it does the trick.

I go down the hall to the office and open our desktop computer. Once it's booted up, I open Google, which tells me that memento mori means "remember that you must die." The snake eating its own tail is an ouroboros, an ancient symbol for infinite renewal. Endless continuity. Infinity.

I Google Jacob Haynes and the *Black Lake Echo*, trying to find the article I'd seen at the house, but the date–1996–is too far back. The *Black Lake Echo* closed down in 1996, shortly after Jacob Haynes died, and their past articles don't appear online. The article I found on top of Annie's dresser must've been a copy of the original.

I hear a sound from the hallway and turn, my chair creaking. It sounded like a window sliding open. I stand, my mind immediately jumping to Leah's text this morning.

He's out.

My heart is thumping wildly. He couldn't have found me. Could he? And *would* he? I never responded to his letters; had eventually contacted the warden, who'd confiscated them. But I'd been told he was clean now. On the right meds.

I look around for a weapon, but all I find is a large octopus-shaped paperweight. I grasp it and creep down the hall. I open the bedroom door, then the bathroom door quietly, but there's nothing. Only one room left to check.

The door to the spare bedroom, the nursery we're hoping to fill, is unlatched. It creaks when I push it open, a long, slow sound that sets my teeth on edge.

I can see immediately that nobody is in here. There isn't enough furniture to hide behind: no bed, no dresser. Just large, unpacked boxes.

But the window is open.

I cross to it and peer outside at our back yard, the recently mowed patch of grass, the wisteria climbing the trellis that leans against the house, the tall oak tree at the back, the patio furniture and barbecue we just bought last weekend.

I set the paperweight down and slide the window shut. Mac must've opened it earlier, I tell myself.

I go back to the office and stare at my half-eaten sandwich, no longer feeling very hungry.

I need to go grocery shopping and get something to make for dinner. I need to do a load of laundry and go to the DMV and change my address. I need to start looking for jobs. Last week I applied as a paramedic with the only private ambulance services in Black Lake, but haven't heard anything yet. I'm not sure I want to hear anything.

Instead of doing any of those things, though, I Google the address for the local library, grab my keys, and head out the door.

The library is on the opposite side of Black Lake. It is small and bright, with huge windows, an oak ceiling and wall to wall shelves. The librarian is a plump, ancient woman with wiry gray curls that poof around her head like a halo, and a lined, smiling face. She tells me she's lived in Black Lake her whole life and remembers the *Black Lake Echo*.

"Went under, like most of the newspapers have," she says, her dry, smoker's voice cracking, segueing quickly into a phlegmy cough.

"Do you have copies of their articles?"

"You mean microfilm? What sort of library would we be if we didn't?" She hefts herself out of her chair and grabs a thick, twisted cane. "Follow me."

I follow her to the back of the library and down a metal staircase into a dark, windowless basement.

"Modern newspapers are made of wood pulp," she says. "It becomes extremely fragile over time. If we don't take care, we could lose all of our history. We store all our microfilms down here in the basement where it's cool and dry."

She leads me to a desk with a large computer-like machine and asks me the date range I'm interested in. I tell her up to the end of March 1996.

She frowns, her gold-rimmed glasses slipping a little way down her nose. "That's a lot of newspaper articles to look through. Why don't we start with the year?"

She leaves, returning a few minutes later with a small box of film. She shows me how to load the film, snapping a lever down to fix it in place. A bunch of images and print appear on the screen and she demonstrates how to reverse, go forward, and zoom.

"The microfilm can't be searched like a computer. You gotta scroll through and just look for the articles you're interested in. This button right here, you press it and it'll print the page. Costs 10c a page."

"Thank you."

"Come upstairs and grab me if you need another box of film."

I thank her again and she leaves, the sound of her cane making muted thumps against the basement floor, slowly receding. I turn to the machine and get to work.

It is tedious and laborious work and my eyes are burning within a half hour of staring intently at the screen. It takes me over an hour, but I find the original article and print a copy for myself. I get back to work, but now I'm not completely sure what I'm looking for. I don't even know the name of the man who was killed today.

I have nothing to go on besides Jacob Haynes's and Annie Jones's names, and even her name–Annie Jones–is probably fake. Thinking back on our conversation, she'd barely told me anything about herself, the conversation staying almost entirely on me.

Honestly, I'm not even sure why I'm doing this. Maybe because I'm bored, no job to go to, nothing to do. Or maybe it's because I felt a connection with Annie Jones. I recognized the fear on her face when she stepped into the house. Whatever the detective said, that fear had been real. Something–or someone–had hurt her in the past. Badly.

I've moved on to another box of microfilm, and then another, before I find anything. It's a short article with Jacob Haynes's name. *Dr.* Jacob Haynes. I scroll back and zoom in, squinting to see the tiny, blurred print. Jacob was a large man with a bulbous nose and beady eyes. In the picture, he's wearing a casual shirt and shorts and a tight smile, standing between two boys in their early teens.

Son Of Missing Local Woman Wins Spelling Bee, blares the headline.

The boy, Jacob Nicholas Jr, appears to be maybe eleven, with a large café au lait mark across the left side of his face. He's holding a certificate in one hand, his mouth twisted into a small grimace. He'd won the town's local spelling bee and gotten a write up in the local paper, although the short article hints at his mother's disappearance two years before being assumed by locals to be murder.

I zoom in further, focusing on Jacob Haynes. I gasp. Peeping out from beneath the bottom of his right sleeve is a tattoo of the words *memento mori*.

The same words scrawled in blood at the gingerbread house.

The same words inside the snake tattoo on Annie's back.

Chapter 5

Him

Memento mori.

Remember that you must die.

That's what he would say when he locked me in the cage in the basement. The cage was small, just big enough for the cocker spaniel who'd died years before. Just big enough for a small, defenseless boy to curl up in.

No food. No water. Just the hard, unforgiving blackness as I waited, desperate, my cries echoing in the emptiness. I eventually learned not to bother crying. It just made the dehydration worse. Instead I counted down the hours, my throat aching with thirst, the scent of my own urine burning my eyes.

I let the movement of the cargo train I've jumped lull me into a relaxed state. *Clack, clack. Clack, clack.* Every movement, every moment, the train brings me closer to her.

The train jerks lightly, then slows as it begins to climb a hill. My eyes fly open, darting around the black train car. I close them again. Quickly. This space is too much like that one. The cage.

I never knew how long he would leave me there. One hour or ten. He always let me out eventually, but only when my muscles were cramped, my limbs shaking, my mind drifting.

When someone you love becomes the person who hurts you, it does terrible things to your mind. It creates a vast, hollow hole, something that can never, never be filled. I didn't start out bad. Honest. But maybe badness spills over, like ink tipped from an inkwell, spreading out, staining, tarnishing everything it touches. I think there's no coming back from it now. Like a hunk of cheese, I was aged in shit, and now that I've matured there's no returning to that small, fragile boy.

Later, once I escaped and got away from that house, I couldn't bear to be in small places. I slept outside, in fields and forests, squatting with the other homeless, the alcoholics, the mentally ill. We banded together, a group of misfits who didn't trust each other, but needed each other. Some of them had tents.

A guy with young eyes and filthy dreadlocks, who smelled of stale bread and engine oil, offered to let me share his, but I couldn't bring myself to go inside. It reminded me too much of that cage. I slept outside until I was robbed and beaten up while sleeping on a bench, and realized there's a type of safety in being hidden. I stole a tent, then. Set it up and stayed close to the others.

One day, a girl joined our group. Small and dirty, with quick, dark eyes and a feral mouth. Mara, she was called. She was younger than me and reminded me a little of *her*. Mara wasn't repulsed by me, disgusted by my twisted body or the lumps on my skin.

Mara gave me my first oxy. It was the first time I could remember ever feeling free from the pain that crouched constantly inside of me, a poisonous viper always snapping at me.

Mara understood me. Appreciated that she couldn't fix me. She never even tried. For a short time, I was happy. As happy as someone like me can get. I've learned that happiness is like a library book, something you can borrow, but not keep. It's best to appreciate things when you have them because they rarely last.

We went looking for more of those magic little pills. We started breaking into houses when people weren't there, then at night, when they were, looking for anything, everything that would ease our pain.

After a while, Mara told me about a man back home who'd done terrible things to her. Her mom's husband, she said. The stories she told me filled me with rage. The injustice of it, how nobody had protected her. Looked out for her. Just like they hadn't looked out for us.

After Mara killed herself, I found the man who'd done all those terrible things to her. He was a very bad man. Very bad, indeed. It turned out Mara had a sister. When I got there, he was standing over her bed.

His pants were down, pooled around his ankles, his butt a white glow in the moonlight. "Now," he growled.

The girl was whimpering, her face turned to the side, eyelids pressed tightly together.

Horror and disgust swelled inside me. And people say *I'm* a monster.

I couldn't see the man's face, but when he grabbed the girl by the throat, blood roared in my ears. Red filtered over my vision, blinding me. I lunged, shoved the man to the ground and used a baseball bat I'd found downstairs, bringing it down on his head over and over again until the man was no longer moving. No longer making a sound.

The blinding red was soon replaced by real red. Red splattered all over the floor, the white sheets on the bed, even the girl. She was wailing behind me, her eyes glassy and wild. I tried to explain that I'd saved her, but she was screaming too loud to understand.

Get out of here.

You've done it again.

The voice was *hers*.

Outside the window, clouds skittered over a dark sky. Moonlight caught on glossy leaves, turning them white as bone. Naked boughs scraped against the building, taunting me. The man on the floor made a faint, groaning sound, blood gurgling in his throat, bubbling out of his fat lips.

I lifted the baseball bat and stepped toward him.

***

After I went to prison, I got clean, but with the lack of drugs came pain. I lived with it. Mostly. Nowadays, as my condition has worsened, I've been prescribed a lot of drugs. Even legal narcotics. Figures, right?

I was inside for a long time. A lot of years to think about the things I'd done. About where I came from. About the people I've hurt.

She came to visit once, shortly after I went inside. The story was big news for a while. Turned out the guy was a big business exec. Rich. Well known. He went to work every day wearing his fancy suit like a disguise. Like a game of dress up, choosing a different character to show the outside world, hiding behind his money, his clothes, his faux philanthropy. But underneath, he was something else entirely. He was pure evil.

The scariest monsters are always the ones hiding in plain sight.

After she came to visit, I only heard from her one more time. She wrote to me, a letter explaining why she couldn't see me anymore. But that letter is how I know where she is. That's how I know where to go now.

The good thing about getting out of here is you can choose to be a new person, Nic, the prison counselor had said. *No matter where you've come from or where you've been, you get to write a new story now.*

I need a new story. I can't go back. Not to that place. Not to the me I was in there. Not ever. Sometimes we have to become different versions of ourselves to fit the story that's already been written for us, but now I have to change it. To change myself and where I go from here.

But I can only do that with her. The only person who's ever loved me for me.

We can start over. Together now.

This time I won't let her go.

Chapter 6

Jess

Mac gets home from work just after 6 p.m., one of the benefits of working at a small, family law firm rather than a big, corporate one in New York. I'm in our large, sunny kitchen, fresh ingredients for street tacos laid out across the island. I've combined the lime juice, soy sauce, garlic, chili and cumin and am searing the beef, fresh from the local butcher, when I hear the front door open.

"Honey, I'm home!" I can hear the smile in Mac's voice at the domestic scene we're enacting.

"Hey, Babe."

"It smells amazing in here!"

He sheds his jacket and hangs it on the back of a chair. His tie hangs loosely around his neck, a bright flash of blue that matches the detergent blue sky outside the window. It's early enough that birds are still singing cheerfully, the late spring sunshine filtering into the room, leaving buttery little patches cast over the pale oak hardwood floors.

"Just in time."

He wraps his arms around me, nuzzling my neck. I twist so I can kiss him fully, then nod at two glasses of crisp Vinho Verde sitting on the island. "Can you take these and set the table?"

Mac does as I ask, then grabs plates and cutlery while I finish searing the meat. We take little bowls and plates of taco fixings to the table and sit across from each other.

"How was your day?" he asks after he's plowed through two tacos. His face is flushed a deep pink from the extra chili he heaped on, one of the cute little quirks I love about my husband.

"You won't believe this," I say, then launch into the story of my day: meeting Annie, finding her naked by the lake, then following her to her house and finding the body of a dead man inside.

"It was *insane*, Mac. Like something from a horror movie or a thriller or something. I mean, I've seen crime scenes, but this was *soo* bloody. And that isn't even the craziest thing. After meeting her this morning, I thought Annie lived there. That the man was her husband. But just before I left, I heard one of the cops talking to the detective, and he said *the man's wife* was on the way. Annie wasn't even his wife!"

Mac has stopped chewing and is staring at me with wide eyes. "Jess, this woman probably killed him!"

"I know. It's crazy. I found this article upstairs when I was getting her some clothes..."

"Wait, you went *inside* the house with her?"

"Well, I didn't know she might be a murderer at that stage. Anyway, there was this article on the dresser about a guy who killed himself in that house, the gingerbread house, in 1996."

"The gingerbread house?"

"Yeah, you know the one you told me about with the ghost of a soaking wet woman who haunts it?"

"But that's only an urban legend. A childhood ghost story."

"Turns out it's kind of true. I mean, not the ghost haunting part, but a woman really did disappear, suspected to have been murdered, drowned in the lake, and years later, her husband killed himself, too. Anyway, I went to the library to find out more about it. The guy who committed suicide has a tattoo of the same words that are on Annie's back *and* were written on the wall inside the house. I think there's a connection."

Mac pops the last bite of taco in his mouth, his face troubled. I reach across the table and grip his hand. He stares at our hands, our wedding rings, the cool white metal against white metal.

Ever since the attack, Mac's been worried about me. It's not like I'd never experienced anti-social behavior before. People in pain, people on drugs, people at the worst moments of their lives—paramedics see it all and sometimes take the brunt of it. He knows I can handle myself; that I'm strong and capable. But this time it was personal. I'd let someone down, and Mac knew I was struggling, mentally if not physically.

Mac runs a hand over his hair, making it stand on end. "Why is this so important to you?"

"You should've seen her face when she went into that house. She was scared of something, Mac. If she killed that man, there's a reason. Somebody needs to find out what it is."

"That's what the police are for. It sounds like this woman is dangerous. The whole situation is dangerous. Isn't that why we left New York?"

"No, we left New York to find a peaceful place to raise our children. And a house with two bathrooms." I smile to show him I'm joking. "Look, Annie *called* me. She called me and I didn't answer. Maybe I could've helped her. You can't ask me to stop helping people, it's part of who I am."

"I know. I'm sorry, I'm just worried. After what happened..."

"I know, I get it," I say. "Life is scary, it is, but I can't run away every time I'm scared. I could die just walking out our front door. Or just staying wrapped up in our rocking chair, too."

"Jesus, that's grim."

I stand and come around to his side of the table, sliding onto his lap.

"My point is, we can't run from the world. We can't hide away and still live. That isn't really living. Black Lake is a new start for me, but I'm not running away again."

"I know, just...be careful. I love you."

"I love you, too."

I lean closer, my lips finding his.

This man, he is the love of my life, and I'm *glad* to be here with him. I am. Mac and I met at a bar in Boston. I was there to see my sister, who introduced him to me, waggling one eyebrow suggestively behind a curved palm.

Mac was this long-limbed guy with shaggy blond hair and a wide, white-toothed smile. He looked like a surfer, not a law student, with his scuffed Converse and his beaded leather bracelet. It turned out his niece had made it for him, which I found endearing. He had a nice energy about him, gentle and easy. I've always been sensitive to people, to their energies, and his was good and pure, a comfortable confidence about him.

From the start there was something about Mac that made me want to lean a little closer. He made me believe in love, made me feel like I could live in a cardboard box under a bridge, as long as he was waiting there, face alight, when I got home at the end of the day.

It was like finding my way home.

Mac returns my kiss, pulling me tight against him. I wrap my arms around his neck, my heartbeat ramping up, my breathing quickening.

When I break away. Mac's face is even more flushed, and no longer from the chili.

"Later," I promise, a seductive smile on my lips. "Dinner first."

Mac groans and reaches for me. "I prefer dessert first."

I can't resist him. We've been married a few years now, but sometimes it feels like it's only been a few minutes.

I hope this feeling never ends.

Mac picks me up, his lips still on mine. I wrap my legs around his waist and he carries me upstairs to our bedroom.

It's only later, as I'm falling asleep, that I remember. In the chaos of the day I forgot to call Leah back about her text this morning.

He's out.

***

The next morning, after Mac's gone to work, I call the number on the business card Detective Rivero gave me. I'd been planning to tell him about what I found out at the library yesterday, but he doesn't answer, so I leave a message asking him to call me back.

I stare for a moment at the two articles I printed at the library yesterday. Both had been written by the same journalist. Jack Walker.

Once again, I'm back in the office opening Google.

Jack Walker is now a Pulitzer Prize winning journalist for the Boston Globe. I immediately send him an email, explaining about the murder in the gingerbread house, and leaving my cell phone number.

I go downstairs, my bare feet cool against the hardwood floor. In the kitchen, I put a pot of water on to boil. We don't have a kettle yet, but I need my morning coffee. I pull open the curtains and let the light flood inside as I pour hot water over Nescafe granules. I take my coffee to a sunny spot in the living room.

I'm catching up on the news on my phone when it rings, the private ambulance company calling to see if I'm interested in interviewing for the position. I'm honestly not sure I am, or that I even want to be a paramedic anymore, and maybe that's why this is all so hard. I've always been the straight arrow, a good head on my shoulders, always knew exactly what I wanted. Except now I don't.

But I don't say any of that out loud. I arrange the interview for Friday late afternoon, hang up, and text Mac. He calls me almost immediately and congratulates me on the interview.

"Are you absolutely sure this is what you want?" he asks.

"It is," I assure him. "I think."

"There's no pressure for you to go running straight back to it. Take some time to find the job you really want. I just want whatever's best for you."

"Thanks, Babe."

My phone beeps a text and I say goodbye to Mac. The text is from Jack Walker asking if we can meet for lunch today. He's in Black Lake visiting family. He names a place in town near the lake.

I'll be there, I text back.

Two hours later I'm walking into a small neighborhood café called the Books a Latte Café. It's stylishly decorated, that sort of bookish, academic look about it, with dark wood and leather chairs and ancient velvet, one wall entirely decked out in mahogany bookshelves with rows and rows of books.

Jack Walker sits at the back, a bowl of vegetable soup and a half sandwich in front of him. He's gained some weight and has a little less hair, but I recognize him from his photo on the newspaper website. He stands and shakes my hand, offers to order me a coffee, which I decline.

"Interesting that you emailed me today." He settles large hands on either side of a yellow mug. "I'm visiting my mother."

"That's good timing."

"You said in your email somebody was murdered yesterday up on Lakeside Road?"

"Yes. And you covered the story of the kids who went missing after Jacob Haynes died?"

"Jacob Haynes." He says it like he's exasperated. "I lost years to that fucking case. Destroyed my marriage, lost my kids, the newspaper shut down and I lost my job. I never got the answers I was looking for."

"You kept investigating even after the newspaper shut down?"

"Yeah. Something didn't add up about that story, the missing wife, the suicide, the kids going missing. I was obsessed with it, sure I could find out the truth. My wife gave me a choice, but ultimately, I decided I had to focus on being great at the only thing I'm actually good at, rather than good at what I was bad at. And I was a terrible husband."

"Well, you won a Pulitzer later, so maybe it's a good thing you let that story go."

"Maybe. I guess I'm just that type, so tenacious I've made it a thing. I fall down, get up, step in shit, and keep on going." He shoots me a crooked smile. He has a nice smile, I think. A nice face. But he's tired. Worn down from life. I can see it on him, the soft things that bruise like fruit.

"So tell me a little more about this woman at the crime scene?"

I tell him about Annie, what she looked like, the tattoo on her back. How she said she was from Paraguay. I think of her accent, what Rivero said. That she could've been wearing a disguise. Maybe even her accent was fake.

"Jacob Haynes was an evil fucker," Jack tells me. "After he died, the police found cages in the basement, collars the size of a child's neck. Leather whips with blood on the ends. There were reports of people hearing children crying. They theorized he killed himself because the kids went missing and he thought they were going to turn him in.

But the kids never showed up. *Anywhere*. I had a different theory."

"Which was?"

"That he'd killed them first, then himself. But I could never prove it."

He sounds furious at this. Barely contained fury. Which makes sense, considering he blew up his life trying to prove it.

"One interesting thing that came out," he says, "was from a woman called Sarah Parker. She was the sister of Jacob Haynes's wife, who'd gone missing when the kids were small. Sarah told me she'd never believed her sister, Mandy, had just walked away. She would never have left her kids behind. Anyway, she told me she'd stopped by one day when Jacob wasn't there. She'd talked her way inside, to see her nephews, and the littlest, J.J., let slip that they had a new sister. That was when Jacob came home and kicked her out."

"A new sister?"

"Yeah, but Sarah said there were no baby things around. When she was leaving, she saw someone peeking out of the blinds upstairs. It was a girl. She said it was hard to tell her age, but she guessed maybe fourteen to sixteen years old."

"A girl," I breathe. "Did Sarah go to the police?"

"Of course, but they never found a girl. And they couldn't do a formal welfare check without the children appearing to be in trouble, which they didn't. They went to school, they were fed. If they were hurt, beaten, the bruises were hidden. On the outside, nothing appeared to be wrong. So nothing was ever done. Sarah was basically ignored."

"How sure was she?" I ask. "Of what she saw?"

"Very."

"That girl." I bite my lip. "I wonder if it was Annie."

Chapter 7

Him

I travel at night and sleep during the day. In the woods, in abandoned houses in empty, old barns.

I spend one rainy night on an empty boat docked in a gurgling river, thunder booming in a dark and feral sky. I stare at the water, pocked with raindrops, eating straight from a can of expired beans I found in a cupboard, and remember another night, a dark and stormy night much like tonight, when an old man, homeless, off his face on drugs, tried to steal my things. I remember watching his body float, face down, in the murky water, the broad reeds and spidery fairy ferns dragging him down to his final, watery grave.

I know I'm hideous and that nobody will help me. One look at my face will only provoke questions, so I stay out of sight. I keep an old balaclava over my face, gloves on my hands, the collar of my coat turned up. I look like a thief, like a hoodlum, but it's that or a monster, and of the two, I choose thief. I steal an old, used car and drive until it's out of gas, then I continue on foot.

The hardest thing to deal with is the hunger. I scavenge in trash cans, terrified of eating poisonous berries in the forest. I drink out of empty planter pots and cracked gutters.

After a few days, I arrive in a small, rural town surrounded by fields and farmhouses. My stomach is empty and I feel dizzy. I need food. Water. My feet ache. Every part of me hurts: my back, my hips, my feet. My shoulders and neck ache, hot waves of pain running along every nerve ending.

In the center of town is a small playground, young children crawling over the equipment like ants on a chunk of sugar. I stop for a moment and watch them.

Until I ran away, I had no idea what other children experienced, that my childhood wasn't normal. Sure, I went to school, and on the surface our family seemed fine, but behind closed doors, it was another story. We weren't treated the way other kids were.

At first his punishments were psychological. Locking us in the cage or telling us someone we loved had died or that our mother had left because she didn't love us. He'd withhold food or threaten to hurt our dog, Bailey. Shit like that. If he did hit us, he knew how to hurt us without leaving overt scars. Only marks that could be covered with clothing.

But that was only the start. The real beatings began later, after *she* arrived.

Her arrival coincided with the tumors getting worse. For a long time I blamed myself. Like he'd brought her to replace me, to find something good and pure to replace the monster I'd become. Now I know it had nothing to do with me. He was haunted by the things he'd done. Haunted by ghosts nobody else could see. He was insane.

I watch the children play, a sharp longing expanding in my chest. The playground is attached to an elementary school and a bell rings. A teacher begins gathering the children, making them stand in straight lines. She stares at me for a long moment, watching me. I turn quickly and limp away, knowing I cut a creepy figure, a suspicious figure, clothed all in black, a balaclava on, even my hands covered.

I find a small grocery store in an old building with a sharply pitched red roof. The front is painted white and it backs up to a narrow alley with a giant garbage can pressed against the back. I lift the lid and a vile scent hits me, rotting meat and vegetables. I gag and tears fill my eyes. I'm so hungry I think I will faint, but I can't eat rotten food.

I hear a thud, then the sound of someone cursing from the front of the store. I press myself into the shadows against the building and slide forward, peering around the corner. An elderly lady has dropped her bag of shopping.

The plastic bag has split and now milk leaks onto the pavement. The lady throws her hands in the air and leaves the groceries, returning inside as she grumbles about cheap plastic bags.

I limp out of my hiding place and gather as much as I can in my arms, then hustle away, around the far side of the store, to the back, and into a little copse of trees.

I slide down onto the ground behind a thick tree trunk. Milk has dribbled down my front. I tip the plastic container and guzzle what's left, then shove the strawberries into my mouth, great handsful. After that, I rip open the bag of crackers and cram them into my mouth.

I can't do anything with the eggs, so I leave them to the side, a meal for a starving fox, perhaps, but there's a small pot of potato salad that I rip open, scooping chunks of flavorful potatoes and crunchy onions into my mouth with my bare hands.

There's also some sort of a bottled shake, green and gloopy, a little like the shakes I used to make for my father to calm his nerves. Or so he thought.

Even in the state I am, I don't touch that. I leave it, moving deeper into the forest. I find a felled, half-rotted tree log and slide inside. I sink into the dirt and leaves, curling onto my side, and finally, finally, go to sleep.

When I wake hours later, the light has started to slope toward the ground, particles of dust hovering in the air. My clothes are stuck to my skin, clammy with sweat. The scent coming from my body is ripe. Sharp.

I sit abruptly. My fingers are tingling and a horrible ringing fills my ears. Even sitting down, I feel off-balance, the world around me spinning. I blink, try to shake my head clear. This was always going to happen; the tumors growing, crushing tissue, squeezing nerves. Pain slices through me, taking my breath away. I let it wash over me, cresting and falling, until I'm finally able to stagger to my feet.

A bird calls from somewhere in the trees and squirrels play in the gathering evening as I limp back to the elementary school. The children have gone home; most of the teachers as well.

I didn't see her earlier, but that doesn't mean she isn't here. I wait behind a large line of trash cans, keeping my eyes on the front door. Eventually, a man comes out. He's in his fifties, clean-shaven with a wobbly stomach, a domed, half-bald head, and the pasty skin that comes from pushing papers all day. He's wearing a navy blazer, a collared white shirt, a striped tie. The principal, I'd guess. Perfect.

I take my balaclava off and follow him to his car. As he bends to open his door, I press a small piece of a blackened stick I found in the forest to his back. Through the material of his blazer, he won't know it isn't a real gun.

"Don't turn around," I tell him. "Do as I say and you won't get hurt."

His hands raise slowly, fear rising off him in waves. "Okay. It's okay. Whatever you want."

"Back inside."

I follow him as he makes his way across the parking lot, through the front doors, into the school's reception.

Once we're safely inside, away from prying eyes, I slip my fake gun into the back of my jeans and stand in front of him. His eyes widen with a flicker of fear as he sees my face.

I know I'm a monster, but it doesn't feel good seeing people react this way. I wish I was normal. Wish I had an ordinary face, a nice, average face, or even a rather boring one, like this man's. Anything but what I have. Sometimes I wonder who I would be, how I would've turned out, if I had been different. But that isn't how life works. It chews you up and then it keeps chewing you up.

We are what we are. Children grow into what they're told they are, they are a reflection of how they're treated. And here I am.

"I need someone's address."

"I can't give out personal information," the man says stupidly, as if I won't hurt him if he doesn't.

A wave of rage washes over me. My hands tighten into fists. The man is small. Defenseless. A mass of soft flesh and jiggly fat. It would take nothing to wrap my hands around his throat, to watch as he thrashes, gasping for breath...

No. I stop myself. I can't kill him. I need to find *her*, and this pathetic, weak-chinned excuse of a human isn't going to stop me. I can control myself. My anger. I'm stronger now.

I step closer to him, let him get a good look at the gnarled tumors on my face, the lumpy, deformed skin, the intensity in my eyes. So he knows. I'm not fucking around.

The scent of his fear is sharp, like burnt paper. He swallows but straightens his shoulders.

"No," he says, more firmly this time. "I can't."

Maybe he isn't as weak as I thought.

I laugh, slow and nasty, the sound destructive.

"Then I'm going to enjoy what comes next."

Chapter 8

Jess

I leave Jack at the café to finish his soup and sandwich and walk through the parking lot, thinking about what he said.

"If the girl at Jacob Haynes's house was sixteen, she'd be in her thirties now."

The woman I'd met–Annie–couldn't have been more than early to mid-twenties at most. She was wearing a lot of makeup, I remember that. But it doesn't seem possible to lose ten years just with makeup.

Surly gray clouds have rolled over the sky, the mercurial spring weather turning cold, sharp rain spitting against my face. I gather my keys out of my purse and press the alarm button, unlocking my car door.

But as I get closer, I stop abruptly.

My tires have been slashed. All four of them.

I stare at the car, dumbfounded. Rain has started to splatter my jeans, my white tennis shoes, my battered leather jacket. A sickening sense of danger hangs in the air, rolling with the unsettled clouds.

I look around, stomach tight as a fist. Has he found me? Is he here?

I dial Leah's number with shaking hands. Across the road, there's a pack of moms outside a school, waiting to pick up their kids. A sensation prickles over my back and I whirl, peering across the small parking lot, into the gray light. I think I see movement, the sway of long, chestnut hair, dripping wet in the rain, a white dress, but then it disappears and I decide I imagined it.

Leah's phone rings and rings. Leah and I met while we were doing the paramedic course together. We became good friends during the few years we worked together, but the hours and the stress and the abuse aren't for everyone. She got pregnant, got married, and gave her notice, before leaving the city and settling in a sleepy suburb.

Now she works at an elementary school in a small town outside of Concord.

"This is my chance to make things right," she told me before she left. "I was pregnant before, you know. I was young. Too young. I had to give her up. But I can do things right this time around."

She's still in touch with a lot of us from her paramedic days. Leah is the connector, the mother hen, the protector, always keeping an eye on us, bringing us together.

Finally, the phone kicks over to voicemail. "Hey Leah. Calling you back about that text. Have you found out anything else? I need to..." I swallow, fear swelling inside me. "I need to know more."

I hang up and look up at the sky. "Fuck!"

"Wow. Bad day," a voice says behind me.

I whirl around. Jack has come out of the café. He surveys the damage to my car. "Somebody have a vendetta against you?"

I stare at the wet pavement, trying to make sense of everything.

"Probably just kids," I say. But my voice sounds thin and high, and a weird, throbbing nausea is spreading straight from my stomach to my head.

Jack nods, something loose and gray passing over his face, like pity. "Probably."

I can tell he doesn't believe it.

"Where do you need to go? I can give you a ride."

"Thanks, but I'll stay here and wait for a tow truck."

He hands me his business card, thick cream and embossed black letters, and tells me to call if I need anything.

The breeze is spiny, the sky troubled, clouds boiling over the water in the distance. I get in my car and call the tow truck company. Rain thumps against the roof. They can't come for over an hour. I growl in frustration. It's too long to wait, but not long enough to leave.

And then I see a car I recognize drive by. Detective Rivero. He slows and pulls up next to what looks like a bar. *Sammy's*, it says in pink fluorescent letters.

I get out of my car and jog toward the bar, dashing between raindrops. To my left, the lake huddles black against a charcoal sky, trees waving and dancing along the shore. I pass an old clapboard church and continue.

Noise floats out from the two-story wooden structure as someone exits the bar. I slip inside Sammy's and am hit by the smells of old leather overlaid with stale cigarettes and ancient booze. It's surprisingly busy, day drinkers mixed with the lunchtime crowd, sitting in cracked vinyl booths and mismatched stools.

My eyes scan the room until I spot Detective Rivero at a table near the back. He's talking with a grizzled older man with wild gray hair and a full-on wizard beard, gesturing wildly, his expression animated.

"Detective Rivero?"

His eyes skitter over me, not recognizing me at first. Then: "Jessica Lambert. That's right."

"It's just Jess."

"Okay, just Jess, this here's Sammy." He motions at the wizard guy, who welcomes me to town. We chat for a few minutes, light banter about moving and living in a small town. He's the owner of the bar and has lived here since he was a kid. After a minute, he excuses himself and returns to the bar. Detective Rivero turns to me.

"Everything okay? Were you able to give your witness statement?"

"What? Oh. Sorry, not yet. I was going to this morning, but..." I roll my eyes. "It's been a crazy day. Someone slashed the tires on my car."

His eyes widen. "Seriously? Where'd this happen?"

"Just down the road. The Books a Latte Café. I'm waiting for a tow truck driver now, actually."

"I'm sorry to hear that. And you just moved here, right?"

I nod.

"That's not a very good welcome to town at all. Here, have a seat." He motions at the seat across from me, his white shirtsleeve lifting, exposing the *Semper Fidelis* tattoo on his left bicep.

I sit across from him, folding my hands on the table.

"Want anything to drink?" he asks.

"I'll have a Coke, thanks."

He motions for Sammy, who brings over a tall, sweating glass of Coke.

"Actually, I'm glad I saw you," I say. "I wanted to talk to you about something I learned about the case yesterday."

"Which one?"

I stare at him hard. His face cracks and a smile softens his hard features. "Just kidding. The murder yesterday, yes?"

"Yes."

"So what'd you learn?"

I shake my head. "Uh uh. You first."

Detective Rivero stares at me, his eyes going flat black. His phone buzzes on the table, rattling against the wood. He glances at it, then away, giving me his full attention. "I'm not sure what you've heard, but that's not how investigations work."

"It's to do with the tattoo I told you was on Annie's back."

His eyes narrow, but I've got his attention.

"Did you get an ID on the body? The guy who was murdered yesterday?" I ask.

He shrugs. "We have a press conference later this afternoon, so you'll hear all this then, but what the hell? The guy who was killed is named Leo Carlson. He's an engineer who bought the house with his wife, Jane, an administrator at the hospital, a few months ago. They moved from Seattle, where they were renting. The house had been sitting empty for years. Before that it was owned by a rental company. We're doing a full background workup on both of them right now."

"He was stabbed." It's a statement, not a question. I saw the damage.

"Multiple times," he confirms.

"Do you have any suspects?"

"Only the one."

"Annie?"

"If that's in fact her name." He assesses me with that calm watchfulness I recognize. "Your turn."

"You aren't playing fair." I take a sip of my Coke. "You're only telling me stuff you're already going to release."

"And you haven't told me anything."

"Okay," I concede. "Here's the tattoo I saw on Annie's back."

I pull the piece of paper with my sketch out of my purse and push it across the table to him. "And this is an article I found in the library yesterday."

I unfold the article I found about Jacob Nicholas Jr. winning the spelling bee and hand it to him, tapping on Jacob Haynes's arm. "He has the same words tattooed on his arm that Annie had on her back. Memento mori. The same words written in blood on the wall inside the house."

Detective Rivero stares at the two pieces of paper. "How did you find this?"

"I saw the article in the bedroom yesterday. The one I told you about from the *Black Lake Echo*. It was just sitting there on the dresser."

He frowns, smoothing a hand over his bushy hair. "I checked with my CSI team. There was no article on the bedroom dresser."

"What? Yes, there was, I read it. I put it back, though. It was from the *Black Lake Echo*, March 21, 1996. After Jacob Haynes killed himself, his two teenage sons went missing and there was an appeal to find them."

"Maybe she took it. Like the coffee cup and the hat and dress."

"It was there, I swear. Here." I rummage in my purse and pull out the other article I'd printed at the library yesterday. "It was this one."

He skims the print-out of the article I found at the murder scene yesterday. "These boys weren't suspects. Maybe they were witnesses."

He peers harder at the second article, the picture of the boy winning the spelling bee. A muscle in his jaw twinges. "It's impossible to see if either of these kids have a tattoo, but that tattoo–*memento mori*–was found on Leo Carlson's body as well." He skewers me with a laser-sharp look. "Now *that* information definitely isn't being released."

I mime zipping my lips shut and throwing away the key. "So they all had that tattoo: Jacob Haynes, who killed himself in 1996; Leo Carlson, who was murdered yesterday; and Annie, or whatever her name is. There must be a connection."

He's still staring at the article. "She must've moved the article. Before we got there."

"Who, Annie?"

"Or whatever her name is."

"She was already gone when I came downstairs. She wouldn't have had time to leave, come back, sneak upstairs, and leave again."

He ponders that for a minute. "Unless she didn't leave."

I think of that flash in my peripheral vision. I'd, annoyingly, thought of the ghost Annie had said haunted the house. But maybe it was just Annie. "I suppose she could've snuck upstairs without me noticing. Maybe hidden in one of the other rooms, then once I went downstairs, went into the bedroom and took it away. Did you find a picture of two young boys and a girl in the underwear drawer?"

"A gun. That's it."

"She took that, too, then. There was a framed picture when I looked. But why?" I say, frustrated. "And how?"

"A secret way out, maybe? It's an old house, filled with all sorts of doors and passageways."

"She'd have to know the house well, but you said it's been empty for quite a while."

This seems to stump him. "Are you sure you didn't know her?"

"Positive. I've never met her before. Why?"

"It just seems like she left the article and the picture for you to see, but then took them away. I wonder if this is personal somehow."

"I just moved here. I don't know anybody besides my husband. In fact, Annie was the first person I've met."

"We'll need you to speak to a police artist. Get a good rendering of her."

"Of course."

My phone rings. The tow truck driver has arrived. I tell him I'll be there in two minutes, then stand.

"There's one last thing," I say, then tell Rivero what Jack Walker told me about Sarah Parker.

"Back in the '90s, she stopped by to see her nephews, but she saw a teenage girl there as well. Except when the police checked in later, there was no girl around."

"Christ." Rivero rubs his head. "This case gets more and more tangled."

"My first thought was maybe it was Annie. Or whatever her name is. But the age doesn't seem right. Annie's too young."

Rivero shakes his head. I can't tell if he's annoyed or impressed. "I can't believe you went and met a journalist."

I check my phone. "Sorry, I've gotta run."

"Listen," Detective Rivero says, stopping me. "That was some fine detective work."

I feel a glow inside me, warm and fuzzy. "Thank you."

"If you ever want a job, I'll be lieutenant one day. Come find me."

I laugh. "That's very cocky."

He smiles but shakes his head. "No. I'm just ambitious and know where I'm going."

"I admire that," I admit. "Most days I barely have a clue what I'm doing or where I'm going."

"'Knowing others is wisdom, knowing yourself is enlightenment,'" he quips. At my confused look, he adds, "The greatest wisdom is always inside you. You'll get there. Listen, there should be some CCTV footage over by the café. I'll make a few calls. See what I can find out about your tires being slashed."

"I appreciate that. I'll stop by the police station later today to give that statement and help the police artist."

"I'll be there. Right now, Jess, you're the only lead we've got."

Chapter 9

Him

I rub the tattoo on my arm, now faded, dimpled, and peaked from the lumps distorting my skin, as I watch the tiny Craftsman across the street. This is the kind of neighborhood where people move to raise families; safe, peaceful. At least looking in. There are basketball hoops in the driveways and bikes left on freshly mowed lawns.

I lean my head against the driver's seat. Pain pulses through me, white hot and glowing. There's so much of it, my whole body is alight, my stomach twisting cruelly.

At least the fat principal had a nice car. After I'd gotten her address, I'd killed him, left his body in the dumpster behind the school, then taken it. I would have to ditch it soon, but at least it got me here.

I scratch at the tattoo, lift a flake of skin with my nail. I stroke my fingertips over the distorted words. I can still make out some of the letters. Memento mori.

Remember that you must die.

It's what he tattooed on us after my mother died. He branded us like cattle to remind us we were his. That we would die.

I had no doubt he would follow through on the threat.

He told us she'd left. That she didn't love us anymore. But I knew the truth. I didn't see him kill her, but I heard it. Heard the muffled screaming, the thuds, then the sound of the front door opening, shutting. When I looked out my window, I saw him carrying something limp and formless across the road, to the lake.

The beatings got worse after that. He starved us. Locked us in the cage. He became paranoid, would just sit there smacking his head with both hands, screaming at my mother to go away, to leave him in peace.

When you're a kid you think these things are normal. You don't question the adults in your life. And later, when we would've happily killed him, he used my brother and me against each other. He made it clear if I told anybody he would hurt Alan. And if Alan told anybody, he'd hurt me. So we stayed silent. For each other.

And then one day he came home with a girl.

She was a raggedy bag of bones, unkempt and filthy, so skinny you could nearly see through her. Her hair was stringy, her nails covered in dirt and grime. She had a crooked nose, a scar on her cheek.

She couldn't have been more than fourteen.

"This is your new mother," he'd said, introducing the girl to us. "You are to call her "Mother" and she will call you both "Son." She will cook for you and care for you. Any help you need will come from her."

Obviously, our father had completely lost it by that point. That was around the time when the tumors had started to form on my body. He was disgusted with me, and, I think, a little afraid of me. Fortunately, it meant he mostly left me alone. He had begun to rely on the health shakes I made for him packed with feverfew, ginger and valerian from the herb garden to soothe his crippling headaches.

As strange as it sounds, those years with Mother were the best I can remember. After years of beating and starving us, my father seemed calmed by having her. She helped allay the ghosts that haunted him. For a short time, anyway. Of course, all good things must come to an end, and soon he started treating her the way he treated us.

Mother wasn't allowed out of the house. He kept her on a long leash inside. Every day when we came home from school she'd be waiting. She'd see us off in the morning, having woken early to pack our lunches and make our breakfast. She helped us with our homework and washed our clothes and made our beds. I think, sometimes, she was the only person who ever truly loved me.

One day, a few years after she'd arrived, I came home to an empty house. No dinner cooking. Dirty dishes in the sink. Laundry still unwashed.

I finally found her in the basement locked in the cage. She was curled into a ball, her arms wrapped tight around her middle. Her face was pulpy, a scarlet mess, her skirt soaked in blood.

She'd tried to run away, it turned out.

"My baby," she'd whispered. "I think I'm losing it."

A flash across the street jolts me back to the present. A car has pulled up out front, parking on the short, gravel driveway. A man gets out, tall, handsome, a runner's build. He opens the back doors and helps two small girls out. He says something and they giggle, their laughter ringing into the cool spring night.

Still no sign of her.

She is close. So close I can almost feel her. And yet she isn't here. I wait one hour. Two. The lights inside go off. Still I wait.

Finally, I get out of the car. I climb the fence, creep through the wet grass, and slip inside, through a window that's cracked open in the kitchen. Shadows tangle with beams of moonlight.

I pause, listening. The sounds of the house fade in: the hum of the refrigerator, the whir of the heating, the tick of a clock. Movement fills my peripheral vision, but it's just a cat, it's eyes glowing in the darkness. It yawns and slinks down the hallway, disappearing through a doorway.

I follow the cat into a playroom, cluttered but neatly organized.

Back in the hallway, I make my way through an archway that leads into an open plan living room and kitchen.

Another wave of pain. My vision blurs. I grit my teeth as a sound comes from upstairs. A creak. My fists tighten, ready to fight.

No. I force myself to relax, my eyes darting to the kitchen window, still open. It could be one of the children. I won't hurt innocent children.

The sound doesn't come again, so I continue my search, looking for something, anything. I start with the bookcase, then move to a sideboard, the TV cabinet, the coffee table drawers. On the dining table, in front of glass patio doors that look over a small, neat garden, I find a laptop charging. When I flip it open, I see a picture of her with the two girls.

The laptop isn't password protected. I scan the folders and documents and images, her Facebook feed, which she doesn't seem to use much. Instagram she uses to post pictures of her family, dressed up for Halloween, grinning happily in front of the Christmas tree.

I go to Chrome and look through her bookmarks, then navigate to her recent search history. And that's when I see it. A Google Alert from earlier in the week.

I know exactly where she is.

Chapter 10

Jess

That night, Mac gets home from work late. I'm already two glasses into a bottle of red wine, sitting on the couch in the living room alone, the lights out, brain working overtime.

Mac knows instantly that something is wrong. He sets his briefcase down on the coffee table and loosens his tie, studying me for a long moment before sitting next to me. I drop my head onto his shoulder and sigh, the movement making the wine in my glass shiver a little, a mini earthquake right there in my hands.

"What's wrong?" he finally asks.

I take another deep slug of wine, then tell him about the tires being slashed.

"The car is at the repair shop now," I say. "It'll be fixed by tomorrow."

He can see I'm stressed and immediately takes me in his arms. "Just kids, I'd imagine."

"Yeah. Probably." I pull away and go to the window.

That feeling is clawing at me, tapping at the back of my neck. But there's no one there. The street is quiet, empty, shadows casting long fingers through the trees.

"Let's go out to dinner," Mac suggests. "It's a beautiful night."

It's late and I haven't even thought about food, so I say yes. We go to a local Italian restaurant Mac says a colleague has been raving about. The colleague is right; the food is fantastic, the atmosphere charming. We have a romantic meal by candlelight, sharing a delicious bottle of Merlot, but I'm distracted and fractious.

After dinner, Mac suggests a walk along the lake. The sun has set, the lake an inky black, dappled with silver moonlight. Tall trees whisper gently as I stare at the water, my mind skittering back to the story Annie told me about the woman who drowned herself beneath the dark waters all those years ago. My eyes unexpectedly fill with tears. What made her do it, walk into the water with her pockets full of stones?

I'm a little drunk, I realize, that dull, fuzzy feeling you get from quite a lot of alcohol, even if it's been spread over a long period of time.

A warm hand tugs at mine, and when I turn, Mac is staring down at me, his brow furrowed. He wipes a tear from my eyes. "Jess, what's going on?"

I break down then and tell him everything, about the text from Leah, and the slashed tires, about that feeling I keep getting that someone is following me, and my fear someone had been inside our house.

"He got out of prison a few weeks ago, Mac. Colin Patterson's out."

There's a heavy beat of silence, as sharp as an elbow to the jaw. Mac's hands on my back tense. "You think it's him? That he's come here?"

"Yes."

"But how in the world could he be out already? And why would he come here?"

"I don't know, but *he told me he would find me*. I just..." I shake my head. "I have this feeling, Mac, and it isn't good."

"He's on his meds now, right? Maybe...maybe he's better now."

I think of that day, the radio crackling, calling us out to a shaggy, gray-haired man hanging like a chandelier off the edge of the Brooklyn Bridge. Colin Patterson was high, meth or heroin, and screaming about bugs feasting on his skin. My partner, Matt, and I finally talked him down, but he'd suddenly leapt on us. He had a knife we hadn't seen in his hands and he swiped at me, catching me on the forearm.

The cut was deep, but nonfatal. I immediately ran for the radio to call for help. But in that split second, I'd left

Matt alone. Colin had stabbed him once in the back before I'd managed to pepper spray him.

I had to choose between restraining Colin and stabilizing Matt. As much as I wanted to choose Matt, I restrained Colin first. It was dangerous not to. I finally managed to get zip ties on Colin, but all the while, my partner was bleeding out on the ground in front of me.

Later, at the hospital, I was waiting outside Matt's room when Colin was rolled past. His glassy eyes had landed on mine.

"I'll find you," he slurred.

Matt's wife Sheila came out then and told me the doctors thought he might be paralyzed. Her face was ravaged, a raw, broken anguish there. I felt like I'd failed my partner. Sometimes, no matter how much you want to, you make no difference at all.

I took some emergency leave, and while I was off, I started getting letters from Colin. That's when we decided to move to Black Lake.

"What did Leah say?" Mac asks. "She's been keeping an eye on him, right?"

"I think so." Leah's good like that. Her brain is like a parole officer's database of where all the bad guys go after prison. "I haven't talked to her yet."

"Call her," he suggests.

"Right now?"

Mac gives me a look. "Uh, yeah. That way we know what she knows."

"She might not know anything," I say as I pull my phone from my purse.

"But she might."

I dial Leah's number, surprised when she answers on the first ring.

"Heya, Jess," she says, sounding harried and exhausted, the chatter of children rising in the background. "Sorry I haven't called back. One of the girls ate a snail, don't even ask, and the other thought it would be funny to draw all over their bedroom walls."

"No problem. Ew. A snail. What'd you do?"

"I mean, it's protein, right? They eat them in France, I'm sure it's fine."

We both laugh. Leah sounds tired, but happy, too. Happier than she used to when working as a paramedic.

"So...he's out," I say.

"Yeah, he's..."

Leah's voice is cut off by the sound of giggling. "Ali, *don't* put your toothbrush in your armpit!" she exclaims. "Sorry, Jess. It's bedtime and crazy here."

"Oh. No problem. Shall I call you back?"

"No, it's fine. So he's gone to his daughter's house. He's staying there for now, with her family. I have the address, I'll text it to you, hold on."

My phone beeps as her text pops through. "There you go."

"Thanks. Got the address."

"I called in a favor to a parole officer I know. His daughter picked him up the day he was released, so he's there now."

"Really?"

Leah must hear something in my voice. "I can't see he would've gone anywhere else. Why?"

"Just..." I glance at Mac.

"Sometimes good people do bad things when bad things happen to them," Leah says gently.

"I don't know."

"I really don't think he's the same guy..."

I cut her off. "Someone slashed my tires the other day."

"It can't be him."

"Why..." I want to ask her why it can't; and why he's been released so early, but then I hear a child crying.

"Oh, for goodness sake. Sorry, Jess, Ali has soap in her eyes, I have to go. I'll call you soon, byeee!"

And then she's gone. I turn to Mac. "Apparently he's staying with his daughter and her family."

Mac wraps his arms around me. "You got the address where he's staying?"

I nod against his chest.

"We'll go there. Tomorrow, okay?"

"Thank you," I whisper.

I slide my arms under his, pull him as close as I can, so there's no space between our bodies. And then our lips find each other and we're making out like a couple of teens right here on the lakeside path. Mac takes my hands and draws me behind a copse of trees, and I know exactly what he's thinking.

My breath catches in my throat as he hikes up my skirt and I tug down his jeans. Then he's hard, buried inside of me, and I'm lost to him, to this desire. We know each other so well, but here in this new town, the stars twinkling brightly overhead, it feels brand new. I watch the depths of his blue eyes, the hard muscular lines of his shoulders, then pleasure rockets through me and my eyes close as I'm consumed with desire. He presses deeper, moaning.

As my eyes open, I catch sight of something just on the edge of the lake's shore. Is it...a person? I can't tell. It's white fabric twisting in the evening's breeze. I squint and for a second, the briefest flash of time, I think I see a soaking wet woman, her long dark hair dripping water all over the ground.

I gasp, a jolt of fear moving through me. Mac thinks I'm caught up in passion.

"I know," he says breathlessly. "Just...wow."

I blink, and the form leaks back into the darkness.

And then it's gone.

And I'm not sure what I saw at all.

Chapter 11

Jess

The next morning, the weather has changed, a storm warning in effect. Anxious clouds boil in a gunmetal gray sky, although the rain holds off for now.

"We have to be back in time for my interview," I tell Mac, as I climb in his car. I've dressed in my only business suit, so I'll be ready no matter what time we get back.

He plugs in the address that Leah gave me and glances at me. "Are you sure you want to go back to being a paramedic?"

"Absolutely." I force a certainty I don't feel into my voice.

A little over an hour later, we pull into a clean, suburban neighborhood. A group of young mothers are pushing strollers down the street, coffee cups in hand, their high ponytails blown about by the rising wind.

I'm glad Mac's car has tinted windows. We park and hunch in our seats across from the house. It isn't long before a young woman with chestnut curls comes outside, pushing an older man slumped in a wheelchair. A little girl of about six walks next to him, grasping his hand. She's chatting animatedly. His eyes are tilted up to hers, a look of adoration on his face.

I study the man in the wheelchair. Colin Patterson. The man who's tormented my sleep for over a year. He looks like he's aged a hundred years.

"Compassionate release." Mac says what we're both thinking. "He must be ill."

I think of what Leah had told me on the phone yesterday. *He isn't the same guy he was.*

"I don't know," I'd hedged.

"Sometimes good people do bad things when bad things happen to them," she said.

"He isn't following me," I say now to Mac.

I'm relieved, of course I am, but confused. Unsettled. I can't shake the feeling there's something out there. Waiting.

I watch as the young woman helps Colin out of his wheelchair, into the back of her car. A half smile floats over his face, his mottled, sunken skin crumpling like crepe.

Colin had a hard life. It came out in the trial. Drugs. Homelessness. Violence. Maybe Leah's right, I realize. Maybe he isn't a bad man so much as a tormented man.

We all have a monster inside of us. We're all capable of bad, but we're capable of good, too. Colin let the monster inside of him get out. But we're each responsible for what happens when it does.

The drive home feels both longer and shorter. When we get back, it's late afternoon and it's started raining, the storm unleashing in earnest. Mac says he'll need to work late tonight to make up for the time off. I tell him I'll grab something to eat at Sammy's before going to my interview. He drops me off outside the bar.

"Good luck," he says. I kiss him and run inside, just as the first drops of rain begin to fall.

I sit at the back and order a Salisbury steak and fries. I have an hour to prepare for my interview, but instead, I pull out the printed article and the notes I've made on Leo Carlson's murder at the gingerbread house.

Sammy brings my meal, glancing at my notes. "Heya, Jess. Rivero mentioned you'd helped a lot with that case the other day." He tuts. "It's a bad business, that house."

"Yes." Suddenly I remember him saying he's lived in Black Lake his whole life. "You'd heard the story before then? The woman who went missing from the gingerbread house?"

"Sure, everyone around here's heard it. My mom was friends with the lady who went missing. Mandy."

"What happened?"

"The official story was that she ran away."

"The unofficial one?"

Sammy hesitates. "It was a long time ago. Lots of rumors. You know, some people think she filled her pockets with rocks and walked into the water."

I recognize this version: it's the one Annie told me.

He strokes his long, gray beard, studying me. "Sometimes raking up the past just brings pain. Are you sure you want to know? You just moved here."

"I'd rather know the truth," I say honestly, because life without truth is hell. I'd rather know the truth than believe a fairy tale.

He sighs, settles himself in the booth across from me. "Tale as old as time, really. Hidden violence at home, a woman who wanted to leave, a man who wouldn't let her. This is all according to my mom. She thought maybe Mandy tried to leave with the kids, but Jacob caught her, killed her. Mandy never would've left those kids."

"Was her body ever found?"

"No. And that's why a murder charge was never made. Jacob said she'd left him; there was no evidence to say any different. After that, he raised the boys, but word around town was he was never the same. The boys weren't either. And then, years later, he killed himself."

"You say the children were boys?"

"Two boys. They went missing after he killed himself, likely so they wouldn't be taken into care."

"I heard there was a girl there."

Sammy shrugs. "I heard that too. One neighbor said he heard a girl crying sometimes, another said she saw a girl running around the back yard. I never saw anything myself."

Someone moves up to the bar and Sammy stands, raps the table with his knuckles. "Gotta get back. Duty calls."

I thank him for his time and dig into my Salisbury steak. It's delicious, flavorful and juicy, the fries perfectly crisped on the outside, light and fluffy on the inside. I'm deep in thought when my phone vibrates with a text. It's an unidentified number.

Meet me at the gingerbread house. I'll tell you everything.

I hit reply: *Annie?*

No cops. Trust me, I'll know.

I'm sure it's Annie. I check my watch. I should ignore the text and go to my interview. At least try to get this job. I look around at the busy bar, Sammy pouring a beer, a waitress bustling past.

Leo Carlson's murder, Jacob Haynes's suicide, the disappearance of Mandy, and now Annie's sudden appearance, it's all connected, I'm sure of it. But how? The only one who knows is Annie.

I think of my partner, Matt, the anguish on his wife's face when the doctors told her that he might be in a wheelchair the rest of his life.

Sometimes we just run out of time. And then all we wish is that we'd done something. Anything. This is a fragile, glass-laid path I'm on, and yet I know I'm not going to sit here doing nothing.

I wipe my steak knife on a napkin and slide it into my purse. Just in case. Then I jot a quick note to Sammy on my napkin, throw some cash on the table, and run outside.

A distant flash of lightning flares in the sky, then thunder, low and distant. The air smells damp, that electric tang that comes from a storm. I yank my umbrella open and dive into the pounding rain. My black shoes and business suit are instantly soaked as I jog toward the gingerbread house.

Beyond the road to my left, gunmetal gray water ripples. Once I reach the house, I skirt the fence and move toward the backyard. The trees are thrashing, wild dancers in the darkening sky. The broken gate bangs in the rising wind. I slip past and make my way to the patio.

The sliding glass door is unlocked. I step inside, shaking rain from my hair. The scent of human decay, of rotting blood, is still thick in the air. My eyes fall on the glass case in the living room, but the ivory rosary has been taken away, marked as evidence, presumably.

"Annie?" I call softly.

Outside, a loud boom of thunder rattles the house.

I move into the kitchen, avoiding patches of dried blood. I hear something from far away, the gentle tinkle of music.

Uh uh uh uh...staying alive...

A creeping sensation crawls up my neck. My darkest instincts ping, and yet I follow them anyway, tracking them like a string of bloody footprints to the basement door.

The Bee Gees song floats through the cracked door. I pull it open. The music grows louder.

"Annie?"

Nothing.

I'm not going down there. No way in hell. But I crouch to peer farther into the dark stairway, just to see what I can see.

I feel it before I hear it. A whoosh of air. An ice cold sensation prickling the back of my neck. In my peripheral vision, a flash of white, and then a blow lands on my left arm. I drop my purse. It's kicked out of the way as I fall to my knees. And then blinding pain as a kick is leveled at my head.

I tumble backward, through the doorway, my fingers grappling to find purchase before I fall down the stairs. I grasp the railing and save myself, but not before the door slams in my face.

"What the fuck!" I shout.

I twist the door handle. Locked. My heart is jack-hammering with terror. Sweat pools under my arms.

And that's when I remember. This door locks from the outside.

I'm trapped.

Chapter 12

Him

It's nearly dark when I arrive, rain spitting onto the spring-warmed pavement. My skin feels like it's burning, the masses inside my lumps writhing, red waves of pain rolling over my entire body, making me sick and dizzy.

I get out of my stolen car and stare up at the old house. It looks bigger than I remember. Bigger, but still menacing. The darkened windows glare back at me. The roof sags more than it used to; the shutters are broken, hanging off their hinges.

I wonder if she's here. If she'll recognize me. Probably not. I am older. Thicker around the waist. My face bloated from the medicine and now mostly covered with tumors. I am not the man I once was.

I stagger through the long grass to the back, to the old gate that's been broken forever. The apple tree still stands tall, its branches dancing in the wind. The house is gloomy. The shadows deep. The darkness clings to me tightly. I can't help the memories pounding at me.

To my surprise, the patio door is unlocked. I let myself inside.

I look around at the splotches of blood, the scent sharp, like iron, taking me back to the day I found Mother locked in the cage in the basement. The day I knew I had to do something. He would kill her, just like he'd killed my mother.

"My baby. I think I'm losing it," she'd moaned.

I grasped her blood-slicked hand through the cage and promised I'd help.

I told Alan what had happened. What my plan was.

I was only a young boy then, just twelve years old. Alan was beautiful, with his bright eyes and his fine, movie-star mouth and his bone-pale skin. But I was clever. I'm the one who knew things. Important things. Like that apple seeds contain cyanide, and in high enough quantities they can kill a person.

We collected as many apples as we could. They'd already started falling that autumn, the soft, ripe flesh rotting in little piles around the backyard.

We scooped the seeds out, collecting hundreds of them. I used my pestle and mortar to grind the seeds into a dry powder, then tipped it into one of the health shakes my father liked so well.

He died a hard death, my father. He screamed at the pain in his head, clawed at his skull until he ripped the skin, great chunks of it falling into his hands. He fell to the floor convulsing, seizures gripping his body.

I hadn't actually been sure I had enough seeds to kill him, but in the end, he found a hammer and ended it himself, smashing it into his own skull to escape the pain.

And then, in the dark of night, we left. Alan, Mother, and me.

I don't regret what I did. I only regret later, leaving her sleeping inside the church. Alan had already disappeared by then, saying we'd be safer if we split up. He was right, but I hesitated because I was weak. Because I was scared.

I knew somebody would help her, but what could they do for a boy like me? A monster with lumps forming on his skin. A murderer. No, we couldn't stay together.

Sometimes you have to make bad choices to protect the people you love. And so I left. But right before I did, she told me her name. Her real name.

And I knew one day I would find my way back to her.

I shake the memories away. None of it matters now.

I'm home.

And soon she will be too.

Chapter 13

Jess

My shoulder aches, my fists are bruised from hammering on the door. But nobody comes. I don't have my phone to call anyone, nor do I have the knife I thought would protect me.

Outside, the storm rages. Thunder shakes the house. The song ends, and for a moment it's silent. That's when I hear a noise. Deep in the basement.

My heart is hammering somewhere in my throat.

The sound comes again. A moan. Like someone is hurt.

"Annie?" I whisper.

I press my hands to the wall, looking desperately for a light switch. I finally find it. A dim light turns on with a faint hum and I move tentatively down the stairs, the wood creaking under my weight. The song has started again.

Huh huh huh huh...staying alive, staying alive.

It's a CD, I realize. I press stop on the player, and the basement is plunged into silence.

There's another moan from the back of the basement. I follow the sound and see a figure huddled in a little ball. A woman. I rush to her, thinking it's Annie.

But it isn't Annie at all.

I stare at the woman, so confused I actually can't speak for a minute.

"*Leah*?"

She tries to pull herself to an upright position, one arm holding the other. Her head is bloody, streams of crimson congealing on her pale skin.

"Where is she?" she croaks.

"Who?"

"She'll kill us." She coughs, blood flecking her lips.

"*Who*? And what the *fuck* is going on? Why are you here?" I kneel and take Leah's arm. She hisses in a sharp breath. Her arm is dislocated, I think.

"Here." I slip out of my blazer, button it, then lower it over Leah's head and insert her elbow into the neckline so it cradles her injured arm. My mind flashes back to helping Annie like this only recently, but I push the memory away.

"I'm so sorry," she whispers, tears mingling with the blood on her cheeks. "I just wanted to get to know her."

"Who?" I help her move over to the wall and lean against it.

Leah looks at me then, and for the first time I see it. The similarity between them. Not so much in the color of her eyes, a soft hazel compared to Annie's bright seafoam green, but in the shape of them, the set of her jaw, the ski slope of her nose.

"Annie?" I breathe.

Leah nods. "You know the daughter I told you I had to give up?"

Puzzle pieces are slotting into place.

"I was pregnant when we escaped this place," she says. "But I was too young. Only sixteen. I knew I couldn't keep her."

"What happened?"

"After the boys left, I found myself on the steps of an old Catholic church. One of the nuns found me there. She took me to a crisis pregnancy center. They arranged the...adoption." She takes a ragged breath. "I gave my baby up, God forgive me. But I swore one day I'd find her. Of course, life happened and I never really got my shit together until that paramedic course where I met you. By then, it sort of seemed too late. But a few weeks ago, Annie found me. She tracked me down through an adoption website. We met. I told her why I'd had to give her up. My whole sordid past. I didn't think anything of it. How furious it might make her. I was just grateful she'd found me."

She swallows. "But a few days ago, I got a Google Alert about the murder that had just happened here. I knew it was Alan. He'd contacted me. Told me he was going to buy this place."

"Alan is Leo Carlson." Another piece of the puzzle clunks into place.

"Yes."

"He thought by buying this place he could exorcize his past," a female voice says behind me.

I whirl. It's Annie, her long, red hair flowing over her shoulders, mingling with something that comes off her like perfume: a sticky, black dust rising, blotting out the pale, flickering light. Evil.

A knife glints in her hand. My breath starts to heave in my chest, my eyes darting behind her. Where the hell did she come from? I didn't hear footsteps.

"Isn't that ridiculous?" Annie continues, and I'm not even surprised to note she doesn't have any accent at all.

Her face has been scrubbed clean. She's younger than I'd thought. Eighteen, maybe nineteen.

"Was it all a lie?" I ask her. "Everything you told me?"

She thinks for a second. "Probably. There's no husband who's a doctor. I'm not a teacher. I'm certainly not from Paraguay. What I *am* is a chameleon. People see what they want to see, after all. Even you, Jess."

Her words hurt, like pricking my ankles on barbed wire. And yet I fell for it, hook, line and sinker. Lonely, cast out from my old life, I'd wanted a friend, and so I'd seen a friend. But it wasn't only my fault. She'd hidden herself from me, covered all the darkest things with a layer of light. People like this, I know, are the most dangerous of all.

"But here's the truth you should be most interested in," she continues. "I did kill Leo Carlson. And I don't regret it."

"But he helped your mother escape. Why would you kill him?"

Annie laughs, a short, evil sound. She looks at Leah. "Do you want to tell her or shall I?"

Leah closes her eyes. "Alan–Leo–was Annie's father. Jacob, for all his flaws, never touched me that way."

Dread fills my chest, a balloon about to burst. "Did he...?"

"Yes. He...he forced me." She swallows and turns to Annie. "He was sorry afterward. He wanted to make it up to me. That's why he helped me escape. And now, my life, it's a good one. I told you that, Annie. You can make more of your life than you think you can."

"You aren't the only one he raped. Trust me, I've watched him. He has a taste for young girls. He deserved to die."

"Maybe," Leah concedes. "But we don't get to be the judge of that."

"I do!" Annie shrieks, eyes blazing. She points the knife at her chest, the blade glinting in the dim yellow light. "I get to be the judge of that! He raped you, then he left you, and *I'm* the one who paid the consequences. You have no idea what I've been through because you abandoned me."

Leah's eyes fill with tears. "Oh Annie, I'm so s..."

"Don't say sorry. It's too late for sorry." Annie whirls to me. "She killed Jacob Haynes. Her and J.J. and Alan. They poisoned him. And Alan, well, you know why he deserved to die."

I feel my mind clear; my focus becomes laser sharp. I've always been good like that, boiling down the moment to exactly what needs to be done. It's only been lately, in the aftermath of everything that happened in New York, that I've felt...lost somehow. Unfocused. But all of that fog lifts now and I am *clear*.

"Annie." I keep my voice soft and level. "What do you want? Whatever it is, we can help you. But you've hurt Leah. We need to get her help."

Annie snorts. "You think I did that? She came here on her own. I was only here to talk to you."

I swing my gaze to Leah. She nods. "It was that Google Alert. I wanted to see if it was true. I heard the music, but the lights were off. I tripped and fell down the stairs."

"The music was for you," Annie tells me.

"Why did you want me here?" I ask.

"I wanted to explain why I killed Alan," she says. "Why I brought you into this. He didn't deserve to die and appear as an innocent victim. Everybody needs to know he's a child rapist. A murderer. I wanted you to know what really happened. To get the justice I deserve."

I stare at her, stunned. "And you think I can get that for you how, exactly?"

She assesses me with bright seafoam green eyes. "Leah told me about you. About what that guy did to you when you were a paramedic. All you lost because of him. And yet you saved his life even though he was trying to take yours. I knew you'd help me when you found me wandering naked by the lake. That's the kind of person you are. You'd bring me back here, get me clothes, and you'd see the newspaper article I left. You'd find out that they're murderers and you'd make sure they got punished."

"Annie." I blow out a big breath, thinking of Colin stuck in his wheelchair. He's been punished. So has Leah. They were victims too. Of poverty. Of drugs. Of abuse. Of life. Maybe we all are to some extent. "If there's one thing I've learned, it's that the past is only in our heads. It's no longer real. All that matters is what you do now. It's never too late to be happy."

Annie's face goes cold and still. "All I wanted was to explain it to you, Jess. Not get a lecture."

I glance at the knife clutched in her hand. She tilts it, looks at it closely.

"This was only just in case. I didn't want to hurt you. Or her." She nods at Leah.

And then she takes a step back, about to slink into the shadows, to leave us, when Leah wrenches herself out of my grasp, jumping to her feet. Her eyes are blazing.

"You *murdered* him, Annie. I'm not letting you go."

I know what she wants to do before she even does it.

Chapter 14

Him

Lightning flashes, wrenching me out of a sleep so deep I'm momentarily uncertain where I am. But as the thunder answers, it all comes back.

I've come home. I've fallen asleep in my old bedroom.

I hear voices somewhere below me. Downstairs.

She's here.

Nothing matters now. Not the pain that holds my body in a vise, not the red siren in my head. Nothing but her.

I get slowly to my feet, my back still hunched and twisted. The muscles and ligaments have all seized up. I can't seem to straighten myself these days.

I stagger down the stairs into the living room. Those words scrawled on the wall mock me.

Memento mori.

I pause briefly and stare at them. For so long I thought they were a threat, a tool my father used to terrify me.

Remember that you must die.

But looking at them now, I see them differently. They are a reminder that every moment is precious. That we should focus on the future, not the past. That death is certain, though its timing is not.

I follow the sound of the voices into the kitchen. The old basement door is open. I don't recognize the voices coming from below.

I peer into the gloom, but can't see the faces of these intruders. Rain pounds on the roof, the windows. Lightning flashes, a giant bolt of electricity beaming through the windows. Thunder shakes the house to its bones.

I know a secret way into the basement. I limp to the pantry, where a hidden door leads to another set of stairs. These stairs are made of stone, slippery and damp beneath my feet. I feel my way through the darkness, muscle memory from childhood taking over. When I reach the bottom, I push the door. It opens silently, as if the old hinges have been oiled.

And that's when I see her.

Older now, of course, but still beautiful, a girl who became a woman. Leah. She's standing next to another woman whose arm is reaching for her, as if she wants to hold her back. There's something on Leah's face, black spilling from her head and streaking down her neck.

Blood? She's talking to a third woman whose back is to me.

"You *murdered* him, Annie. I'm not letting you go."

I inch closer as Annie backs away from her.

There's a brief flash. Not lightning. No. A knife. This Annie speaking to my Leah has a knife. And she's raising it...

I don't think, I act. I lunge at Annie, knocking her aside. She stumbles, the knife clattering to the ground, and turns to stare at me briefly with sea-green eyes. I recognize those eyes. The same green as my father. The same green as my brother.

She takes in my misshapen figure, my deformed, lumpy skin, her eyes going wide with horror. I know what she sees, but I don't care. I won't let her hurt Leah.

Annie scoops the knife back into her hands. Her mouth twists into an evil smile, eyes wild and glittering.

"Hello, J.J.," she says.

And then she burrows the knife into my belly.

Hot, lancing pain burns through my middle. Crimson blood instantly soaks my shirt, seeping onto my hands, slick and sticky. Leah and I lock eyes. She stares at me, her complexion ghost white. Her eyes are like big, black holes, a sheen of sweat covering her skin. I moan and drop to my knees.

Remember that you must die.

I hear my father's voice in my head, an echo of my childhood. Fear burns in my chest, my mouth filling with blood.

Thunder booms again, closer this time. It shakes the house, the stairs.

Annie turns to face Leah, blood dripping from the knife. She lunges, the tip of her blade catching the forearm Leah throws up. The other woman is shouting, telling Annie to drop the knife. But she is powerless to help without being stabbed, too.

Remember that you must die.

Maybe, but not right now.

I stagger to my feet, and lunge at Annie.

Chapter 15

Jess

Chaos comes in an instant.

Thunder cracks as the misshapen, twisted man lunges for Annie. She pivots, stabs him again, this time in the chest. The knife sticks there, looking almost harmless, like a tiny acupuncture needle, but he doesn't stop. He uses his weight to propel her backward. Her head cracks against the basement wall and she sinks to the ground, momentarily stunned, as she's pinned by his weight.

A sickening boom of thunder crashes upstairs, the light dimming, then brightening.

The man wrenches the knife out of his chest, holds it high above his head. He stares at it for a long moment, the pale, flickering light catching the sheen of sweat on his disfigured facing, turning it waxy and alien. And then he thrusts it down, down, down. Annie raises her hands to his forearms, slowing its descent, but she's no match for his strength.

"Stop!" I scream, still holding Leah back. "Stop!"

But nobody listens to me. The knife continues in slow motion toward Annie's throat.

At the last second, I throw my weight against the man, shoving him off her. His scent hits me like a slap, sweat and a wild tang, like burnt socks.

The knife barely penetrates Annie's shoulder, and then she's rolling away, sliding into the shadows like an eel beneath the surface of the water.

Leah kneels next to the bleeding man as the rafters begin to shake, and when I look up, cops are thumping down the stairs, shouting, guns raised. Rivero. Sammy gave him the note I left at the bar.

The cops have their guns raised. I lift my hands in the air, but Leah ignores them.

"Oh, J.J., why did you do that?" Leah is sobbing, her hands slick with blood as she presses her hands to his knife wound.

I have nothing but my shirt now. I yank it off, push her aside, and press it to the man's stomach wound. The blood is bright red, frothy, pulsating from the gash. He only has minutes to live.

"We need an ambulance!" I shout. "This man's bleeding out!"

"Jess." I hear Rivero's voice from far away. "Jess, where is she?"

I look around the basement, my eyes trying to penetrate every corner of shadow and light.

But once again, Annie is gone.

Chapter 16

Jess

It's quiet now, all the violence and chaos behind me.

I am curled up on the couch with Mac, snuggled into the safe, warm embrace of my husband, the fire in the hearth dancing in the gathering twilight. It isn't really that cold, but Mac knows I need the comfort of a fire, a warm embrace, a good glass of red wine, and now I have all three.

"I'm just glad Sammy called Rivero and gave him the note you left," he says, dropping his lips to the top of my head.

"Me too." I twist in his arms and look up at him. "I missed my interview."

Mac tucks a tendril of hair behind my ear, a smile curling the corners of his mouth. "You didn't want to go anyway, did you?"

"I guess...no. I don't want to be a paramedic anymore."

"What next, then?"

I think of what Rivero told me after he'd finally had a chance to sit down and take my official statement.

"I checked the CCTV footage over by the café," Rivero had said. "It was a kid. Fourteen years old. Parents going through a messy divorce. He did it to a few cars that day. We picked him up at his mom's house and scared the shit out of him. He might think twice about doing something like that again. Even in a small town, we get bad behavior, but I'm sorry it happened when you first moved here."

I'm more relieved than he could know. A kid is a lot less scary than an aging, revenge-filled drug addict.

I thanked him and stood to go, then turned to face him at the last minute. "Were you serious about offering me a job?"

Being a detective doesn't jive with the life I thought I'd have. I thought Black Lake would be someplace quiet and calm, a peaceful place to raise the family Mac and I want. But something about it feels right. Like a calling I'd never heard before.

"Absolutely," he says. "Some people just have it, and you do. I'm honestly not sure we would've solved this case without your help."

That warm glow again, like I'd done something useful. Like I made a difference.

"Thanks."

Rivero smiled. "Knowing yourself is enlightenment."

"I didn't take you for a shrink," I joked.

"Naw, a philosopher. A chameleon. Good detectives are shapeshifters. We gotta be able to mix with anybody, be anything, but to be able to do that and get back to yourself at the end of it, you gotta know yourself."

"I want to train to be a detective," I tell Mac now.

He doesn't seem surprised in the slightest.

"I want to put away bad guys like Jacob," I continue. "Bad guys who hurt people. I want to get justice for the victims, for those left behind. For all the Annies and Leahs who never got the justice they deserved."

I think of Leah and Annie and the misshapen man–J.J.–who'd succumbed to his wounds on the floor of the basement he'd spent much of his childhood locked inside. His funeral is tomorrow, a small, private affair that Leah has organized. Mostly for herself. To say goodbye to her past, a past that shaped the woman she became.

"Jacob killed his wife, Mandy. Drowned her in the lake when she said she was going to leave him. He admitted it to Leah. A threat he thought would make her too scared to leave him, too. He was haunted by what he'd done, Leah said, haunted by Mandy. Leah could see him slowly going insane and she became increasingly scared of him."

"But why did she move in with him in the first place?" Mac asks.

"Leah had a bad childhood. Her mom was an addict and she never knew her dad. Just a parade of dodgy boyfriends. She was twelve when she ran away. Jacob found her homeless on the street and offered her a place to live in exchange for being a mother to his children. She didn't realize he meant it literally. The boys were required to call her Mother and she had to make their school lunches, wash their clothes, even read them bedtime stories."

Mac's mouth twists in disgust.

"She said she had no other options, but things went downhill pretty quick," I continue. "He kept her on a leash just long enough to move around downstairs. She wasn't allowed outside. Was only allowed two bathroom breaks a day. Once she realized she was pregnant with Alan's baby, she tried to run away, but Jacob caught her. He beat her so bad she started bleeding. That's when J.J. knew he had to get them out of there. He poisoned Jacob and they all disappeared, eventually going their separate ways, Alan to college, J.J. to prison, and Leah to give birth to Annie, then eventually to paramedic training and her husband, her children."

A flicker in my peripheral vision draws my attention to the window, the blinds that are still open. I cross the room to peer outside. A flash of white, a dress waving in the breeze. Annie, perhaps. Or maybe Mandy?

But then it's gone, and I know I'm being ridiculous. Mandy is dead. I think sometimes my imagination gets the best of me. And Annie, well, despite a national manhunt, nobody's seen her.

But I'll find her. One day.

"You okay?" Mac asks.

"Yep." I snap the blinds shut and return to my husband. I slide onto his lap and wrap my arms around his neck, smile down into his beautiful blue eyes.

And I know I'm exactly where I belong.

Did you enjoy The Stranger At Black Lake?

Then read on for a sneak peek at the first in the Jess Lambert series, These Still Black Waters, as well as the second in the series, What Lies In Darkness.

And make sure to sign up for my book club newsletter to hear more about my books, as well as win books every month. www.Christina-McDonald.com/book-club

These Still Black Waters

Chapter 1

The body cooled quickly on the ground beside me. The night was deep, the woods thick enough that the moon did not interrupt my work. I'd always equated darkness with unknowing. The unconscious, I believed, was unknown until something crossed into the light of awareness. A wood at night, as an example. What was ahead was obscured until you moved close enough for it to be illuminated. But tonight, although I worked in darkness, I knew exactly why I was here.

I'd made my choices.

That's all life was: a series of choices. That was what it all came down to in the end. It didn't just happen. We made our choices. The good. The bad. The mundane. Free will.

We made choices every day, both knowingly and unknowingly. From simple ones like what to eat for dinner to bigger ones like whether to take that promotion we knew would move us across the country. Some choices we regret. Some we are proud of. Losses. Gains. Successes. Failures. Friends. Enemies. We have the power of choice. The only inescapable thing is the inevitability of choice.

In other words, the past may be dead, but it is our choice if we bury it.

I sat on the cold dirt floor next to the body and extracted an item from my pocket. I turned it over in my hand. The colors were dull, the edges covered with dirt. It was small. Too small to carry such destruction. Wasn't it funny how the smallest things could carry the greatest weight?

I closed my eyes and let the past play over the screen of my eyelids. Somewhere far away, I heard the sharp whoop of a police siren. Whoop, whoop. *And the wind rustling in the trees, like the hissing of a snake.*

I needed to leave, but I didn't. Not yet. I listened, the sounds a melody, a rhythm, a poem, and I let myself be carried away until they swelled too big, like the surf, louder and louder, a cacophony of noise. I clapped my hands over my ears, trying to focus on the image of her face. It was the only thing that gave me peace.

If—when—people find out what I've done, I hope they understand that, at least. Why I made these choices. Why I had to do it.

It was all for her.

Later, people might say that I snapped. I lost my mind. Blew up, broke down, went crazy. All the mundane adjectives people use when they don't know the inside of a person.

But that wasn't true. I'd made my choices with a clear mind in the cold light of day. I knew exactly what I did and why I did it.

I often thought of life as an echo. Stand on the edge of any abyss and shout into the dark, your echo will return. What you send out comes back. You could choose to do what was right or you could choose to do what was wrong, but when you chose wrong, rest assured, those ghosts would come back to haunt you.

Choices have consequences. They chose wrong.

Chapter 2

Neve

We don't take much with us when we leave. There doesn't seem to be a point. What nobody tells you about being the victim of a home invasion is you never know when they're coming back. And so we left.

That's why Ash and I stand almost empty-handed in front of the creaking old Victorian house of my childhood summers.

I say "almost" because I'm holding a glossy-leafed plant Eli got me for our ten-year anniversary. Ash named the plant Priscilla years ago, when she was still a cute kid and not an angsty teenager. Priss the pinstripe calathea.

I set Priss on the gravel drive, and we stare up at the house. It looks like something out of a Brontë novel looming above us, a brooding presence with shiny pale bricks and washed-out, jutting attic dormers and dark, spiky turrets. The roof is steep and gabled, the windows long and narrow. The front porch is almost hidden beneath a sweep of ivy that stretches over the brick.

Above the front door in elegant script: *Dullahan House.*

It is different and yet the same. The house. The driveway. The rustling trees. Standing in the harsh, hot sunlight, staring up at it, I feel the strangest thing. A bizarre disturbance in the air. A restlessness. Like when your skin knows a storm is coming, or the prickly waves of something electric wash over you.

"So this is it." Ash looks underwhelmed. "How long since you've been here?"

"Over twenty years. We came every summer when I was a kid. It's been in my family for years."

I have my reasons for not returning after that last summer, but some things are better forgotten than spoken of. Life goes on whether you dwell on the past or not.

"It's nice, right?" I say.

Ash's lips twist, a hand on one hip. "Whatever. I don't have the same disease you do, Mom."

"What's that supposed to mean?"

"You legit have denialitis. Like, *look* at this place! It's totally falling apart."

I look again at Dullahan House. "Maybe it's a little . . . shabby, but . . ."

My voice trails off as I take a second look. The pale green trim is cracked and peeling. Some of the brickwork is crumbling. The wooden porch is listing to the side, the shrubbery a little wilder than it should be. I suppose I see what she means. It has a sort of . . . deserted air about it.

It's the windows. There are too many of them. As if the house is staring at me. Something about it is uninviting, a little stark. A shiver rakes over me despite the midday sun beating down on my arms. Because I of all people know that appearances can be deceiving.

"It's fine," I say, because it is. It's still perfectly pleasing. The jewel- green front lawn has recently been mowed by the property management company. The gravel driveway has been weeded. "It's just not been used much lately."

We've had it available as a vacation rental since my mother went into a care home, but when the pandemic hit, not a lot of people were vacationing.

Ash rolls her eyes. "Whatever."

My body tenses. I wish Eli were here to provide a buffer between us. But now it's just Ash and me and this house, the only place I could escape to after everything that's happened. All we have is what's ahead of us. A new start. A new home. A new life.

"Hey, would you rather have a mullet or no toothpaste for the rest of your life?" I ask as a way of lightening the mood. Would You Rather is something we've played since Ash was little. I like it because, like life, it's a game of choice, and theoretical choices are a lot more fun than real ones.

Ash thinks about this. "A mullet. I could just put it in a ponytail."

I laugh. Down the road, an ornate black gate creaks open, the shrill, metallic shriek carrying fast under the still, hot sun. The gate encloses this lakeside community of six houses, all made with the same grand old Victorian architecture: three, including mine, sitting directly on the lake and three across the street on a slope.

A BMW rolls through the gates and parks in a driveway across from us. The house is smaller than mine but still beautiful with leaded windows and classic Victorian features.

A woman gets out. She is middle-aged and shaped like a carrot, with scowling, argumentative eyes. Her dark hair is scraped into a high, round bun, and she's wearing full workout gear, like she's been to the gym.

A small dog hops out of the car, some sort of Maltese mix with cropped white fur. He catches sight of us and darts across the road as the woman gathers groceries from her trunk. I kneel, my hand extended so he can sniff it. He licks my fingertips and wags his tail.

"Hey, sweetie!" I croon.

I think of my dog back home, Molly, her silky black-and-white fur, her trusting brown eyes, and all the animals at the vet where I worked, and I feel an ache for everything I've lost.

"Toby, come!" the woman snaps, her eyes skittering over us. Toby obediently trots back to her, and a second later, they disappear inside.

Ash turns away from me, her blue-black hair ruffling as a hot gust of wind kicks up. She cut it a few weeks before, a short punk-rock bob with a funky little line shaved into the side. I could tell at the time that Eli secretly hated it, but I liked that Ash was confident enough to pull off something so bold. I think it's brave. *She* is brave. Brave and courageous. The bravest person I've ever known.

An eerie quietness descends. I don't like it. It reminds me that bad things have happened here. At one point in my life, I swore I would never come back, and yet here I am. I wonder, not for the first time, if returning was the right choice.

"You're going to love it here." I sound too bright, shiny as a pearl in the sunlight. "The lake is out back, and there's a beach and a dock and kayaks. Plus, there's all the woods to explore. And there's an old boathouse down by the lake. We can get outside more. Go hiking or swimming. Whatever you want."

This is wishful thinking. Ever since the home invasion, Ash mostly stays locked in her room, where she feels safe.

I'm hoping being here can bring a semblance of normality back to our lives.

Ash's green eyes pin me with a hard glare, forcing me to see the angry red scar the bullet scorched along her hairline near her temple. "Whatever I want except see Dad."

I want to be honest with her, but what's the point when I'm not even honest about the things I've done? I've held my secrets close for so long, they've become like a second skin. But secrets turn into lies when they're spoken out loud, so I measure my reply carefully before giving it.

"It won't be forever, Ash."

So often in parenting, love and guilt are intermingled, nearly impossible to separate. I should do this; I shouldn't do that. It's never clear until you look back. Hindsight is twenty-twenty, as they say.

"The lady from the property management company will be here in about half an hour." I set Priss in the shade of the porch and grab Ash's hand. "Come on. I'll show you the lake."

We push through a path running along the side of the house. Ash's black combat boots, too hot for this weather, crunch over the gravel. We emerge into the backyard, and there it is, Black Lake. The water is lower than I've ever seen it, climate change and successive droughts taking their toll, but it's still there, glistening hypnotically in the sun. A wooden dock juts out into the water, shared between my neighbor's house and mine. Kissing the dark waters is a narrow sand beach that runs for miles in either direction. In the distance, wooded islands dot the lake, towering white pines fringing the shore.

It's exactly as I remember it: beautiful even though so much ugliness happened here.

"Gee, you can really see why they named it Black Lake." Ash's voice is tight and sullen.

"It's the tannin from the trees. It's safe, though, I promise." I point at a path that disappears into the trees fringing the lake. "Let's go for a walk. There are trails back there."

I see her hesitate. She's eager to get inside, to hide away playing *Fortnite* or reading a book or zoning out while listening to grunge music. Before she has a chance to argue, I head for the wooded path. With no other choice, she follows.

We wander the trail, our shoes crunching over dried twigs and pine cones and packed earth. We follow the shoreline and soon come to the boathouse. It's ghostly, derelict, crouched among the reeds. The door is locked, so we carry on, following the narrow ribbon of dirt as it cuts through weeds and bushes.

All around us, the trees are thick and tall, the air clean and fresh, practically humming with birds singing and insects buzzing. The heat on my skin and the beads of sweat sliding between my breasts make me feel alive.

I find peace in the quiet stillness and exhale in one massive breath, the way I used to each summer when we'd finally arrive. Those days when I could take my shoes off and run into the water, slurp on half-melted Otter Pops, and marathon Nick at Nite with my summer friends were the best.

Until they weren't.

We walk for about twenty minutes until we reach a small beach with a felled tree jutting into the lake. Ash unlaces her boots, pushes up her leggings, and walks into the water, one hand pressed against the tree for balance.

The water hits her knees, and there's a small smile on her face. It warms my heart, and I begin to think maybe, *maybe* we'll be okay here.

Ash dives into the water. After a minute, she comes up gasping and laughing, water streaming from her hair. Sometimes the child in her still emerges, the quiet, gentle girl I know. The world is so hard on soft things, I find. On sensitive, bookish introverts like my girl.

"Come in, Mom!"

"Absolutely not!"

She smacks the surface with her palm, sending an arc of water toward me. I jump out of the way, laughing. God, it feels good to laugh!

"All right, all right!" I slip my sundress off and wade in wearing just my bra and underwear. The water is frigid, and I gasp as the chill bites my skin.

"You'll get used to it!" Ash calls.

The bottom falls away steeply, and soon I am underwater. It steals the breath from my lungs, but Ash is right. It is invigorating.

I swim out to Ash, and gradually our muscles warm as we race each other into deeper water and back. We lose track of time, our fingertips wrinkling as we splash in the shallows and float on our backs.

I'm treading water and laughing, Ash bobbing up and down in the water a little way from me, when I start to feel dizzy. It's as if the whole world is tilting, a mudslide that I'm caught in. In front of me, Ash shimmers, a mirage in the bright sunlight.

And then, abruptly, she disappears.

I swim in a circle, stunned and confused.

"Ash?" My voice is shrill with panic.

There's no reply. Adrenaline kicks in my veins.

"Ashley Rose, come out now!"

But she doesn't.

THESE
STILL BLACK
WATERS
A JESS LAMBERT THRILLER
CHRISTINA McDONALD

What Lies In Darkness

Chapter 1

Alice

The Accident—Christmas Eve

My family was murdered at the witching hour.

I know they were murdered, otherwise why wouldn't they have come back? Families don't just disappear. They don't just walk away from the people they love.

That night, there was nothing to make me think something bad was about to happen. No chill skating over my neck. No dark whispers riding the winter wind. No creepy premonition that everything was going to change.

We were happy. That's what I remembered most afterward.

It was Christmas Eve, my favorite night of the year. We always stayed at my aunt Mel and uncle Jack's on Christmas Eve because their house was the biggest. Every year they did a fancy, catered dinner and endless desserts, their house decked out with lights and tinsel and a huge tree with designer baubles, not the homemade ones we had on our tree. We'd go to bed late, our stomachs full, our bodies sleepy, and then, on Christmas morning, we'd roll out of bed early wearing our matching pajamas and run downstairs to open our presents together.

My parents could never afford any of the stuff Mel and Jack did. I'm not saying we were poor, just our presents were, like, pajamas and stuff, not electric ride-on cars or Apple Watches or Gucci socks.

That Christmas Eve, after dinner, somebody turned on some old dance tunes, and the adults, who by that time were hilariously drunk, had started dancing. My grandma was there, too. She'd just arrived from Florida. Mel had hired a Santa to show up for Finn, and I was wandering around snapping pictures.

I had a bit of a sore throat, so my parents decided to take us home instead of staying that night. Dad said I needed a good night's sleep. I remember walking to the car, Mom's good arm, not the one in the sling, wrapped around me. Dad was laughing at something my little sister, Ella, had said. He had a great laugh, his whole face kinda crinkling, his eyes squinting, his body shaking with joy.

Like I said, we were happy. So happy it hurts to think about now.

I stopped to catch a snowflake on my tongue. Did you know in Scotland they have 421 words for snow? A large snowflake is called a skelt, a fine driving snow, a snaw-pusher. This snow was a flukra, snow falling in large blobs.

"Come on, Alice!" Ella shouted. "Get in, it's freezing!"

We piled into the minivan, Ella chatting about something I no longer remember, even though now, in the darkest hours of night, I try my hardest to remember what it was. Makeup, maybe, or boys. They'd already started noticing her, even at ten, with her big blue eyes and her bubbly personality. Ten going on sixteen, Mom always said.

I buckled up, the taste of the snow, cold and metallic, like winter and something harder, like stone, lingering in my mouth. The clock on the dashboard said 11:47 p.m. I noticed because it was so far past my bedtime.

"Pete, do you really think—" Mom began.

"It's fine." Dad's eyes cut to the rearview window, a streetlight glinting off his glasses. "You girls buckled?"

"Yes," we chorused.

Ella was lying. Her coat was draped over her like a blanket, but I could see her seat belt. Empty. Unfastened. I glared at her, hoping she'd feel the weight of my gaze. But she didn't lift her head from under the warm nest of her hood. I didn't say anything, though. I wasn't a tattletale.

Later, I would regret that. I would torment myself with how different things could've been if I'd only spoken up.

Something fluttered in my peripheral vision. Maybe a bat? Or a bird braving the cold. I didn't think about it too much. I felt safe and secure surrounded by my family.

Snow battered the windscreen, the roads already covered. The wipers beat on max, rhythmically shoving at the white flakes. The headlights barely cut through the snow swirling around us.

I was just starting to fall asleep when the car slowed. A couple of construction barriers with a Road Closed sign were blocking the road.

"That's weird," Mom said. "I wonder what's happened."

"Maybe they're fixing some of those potholes," Dad said. "I'll turn around."

"Maybe we should . . ." Mom's voice was pinched with worry.

"This road's closed, honey."

"Pete, I really don't—"

"It's fine." Dad cut her off, a little impatient, a little annoyed. He'd been getting annoyed with her a lot more lately. He'd been getting annoyed with all of us lately. Not anything big, just little things I only noticed after.

That's how life breaks down when something bad happens. Those dark, sudden moments that happen without warning. This was my life before. This is my life now. The two are nothing alike.

Dad spun the minivan around and turned into Killer's Grove.

It was kind of a dumb name. Killer's Grove. I guess years ago, a serial killer claimed he'd been burying bodies there. All you had to do was mention Killer's Grove and people would go, Oh, you mean that haunted road where all the bodies are dumped? And you'd say, Yeah, even though only one body was ever found there, and that was in, like, 1970 or something. And they'd tell you one of the billions of ghost stories everybody knew.

Mostly, those stories were told in a breathless dude you won't believe this sort of way, and they usually started with a bunch of goths staying in Killer's Grove on Halloween while stoned off their faces. It was the sort of dead zone where stories of people going missing were common, where your phone couldn't get a good signal, and if you stood just long enough, you'd feel the cold scratch of something whispering over your skin.

Nobody ever had any specifics, really. Just that the couple of miles of road that stretched through the forest near Black Lake were haunted and had always been haunted.

My dad didn't believe in those stories, but my mom did. Maybe it was the Irish in her. She's the one who warned us about the witching hour.

Nothing good ever happens after midnight, she'd tell my sister and me. That's when all the spirits come out of hiding. When the veil lifts between the dead and the living and the spirits travel between the worlds.

So, yeah, the name was dumb. But still, some things stick with people. The past isn't some sandcastle that can just be wiped away by the tide.

I stared out my window. The road ahead was long and narrow. Darkness had stitched the trees together, a curtain of black. Our headlights barely cut through the white snow swirling like static from an old TV screen around us.

Ancient evergreens dusted with white pushed up over the sides of the winding road, thick branches arcing like gnarled fingers. On either side of the road was forest, miles and miles of it: northern hardwood, white pine and red oak, with jagged chasms and plunging gorges and caves. In the summer, we'd go camping, hike the cobwebbed paths, but now everything was frozen.

My parents were arguing in the front, still doing that thing they sometimes did where half their conversation was out loud and the rest was telepathic. They'd always done it, as long as I could remember. It was totally annoying. I closed my eyes and let their voices merge with the windshield wipers as sleep pulled at me.

"Do you think—" Dad began.

"No."

"Are you—"

"Tomorrow. Honestly, tonight I . . ." Mom sighed.

"I know, I get it."

"It's just, it's Christmas, and I think . . . Pete, watch out!"

My eyelids fluttered at my mom's scream.

There was a flare of something. Light? Shadow? I couldn't tell.

It all happened so fast.

Dad slammed on the brakes, and the minivan skidded, then swerved. My stomach leaped into my throat. Dad cursed, trying to correct. But the tires couldn't get any grip on the snowy pavement, and we veered off the road, clipping a tree with a bone-jarring thwuck. And then we were airborne, metal crunching as the car flipped.

I could hear someone screaming—was it me?—as we spun, inside a washing machine of white snow and black night. Pain ripped through my arm. The metal on the roof screeched as we landed upside down on the pavement. The minivan rocked and then, with a final sickening groan, tipped onto its side, flinging me against my window.

My head cracked against the glass. Blood filled my mouth, poured into my eyes. And then everything went black.

I don't know how long I was out, but when I came to, the only sound was the windshield wipers still going. Swish, swish, swish. Blood, hot and sticky, dripped down my nose, the scent like melting rust. Pain gushed over me in a hot wave. My arm was twisted in an unnatural direction.

The car had landed on its side. My side. Snow dusted my cheeks.

"Mom?" I whispered, my eyes still squeezed tightly shut.

But there was no answer. Only the gentle sound of snow falling and the hiss of the wind and the beat of the wipers.

"Dad? Ella?"

Still no answer.

I opened my eyes. I was lying on the side of the car surrounded by junk: my backpack, a box of crackers, an empty Coke can. I tried to move my head, but pain made me stop. A whimper escaped my mouth. I slit my eyes open again, turning my neck slowly despite the pain and dread and panic filling me. I expected to see Ella next to me, to see my mom and dad in the front.

I was afraid they were all dead.

But what I saw was worse.

Horror gushed in. I started to tremble. My heart hammered. Hot tears filled my eyes. I squeezed them shut, then open again. But everything was still exactly the same.

There was nobody there.

Besides me, the car was empty.

My family was gone.

In my peripheral vision, the clock ticked over: 12:01 a.m.

The witching hour had arrived.

Scan To Read More

ACKNOWLEDGEMENTS

First and foremost, to my readers. Thank you for loving Jess Lambert so much that I couldn't get her out of my head. Your love, reviews and messages meant I kept imagining where she came from and where she is going. From that came book two, What Lies In Darkness, and this prequel novella. So thank you to every one of you who reached out or gave a good review, who loved Jess and wanted to read more about her. This one's for you!

Thank you also to Anne Brewer for her exceptional skill at editing with grace, insightfulness, and style. And to Anna Dorfman for designing such a beautiful cover that I gasped when I opened the file.

And, as always, thank you to my husband, Richard. Without him, this novella never would have happened. Thank you for encouraging me and believing in me, even when I don't believe in myself.

Join my bookclub for chances to win free books and stay up to date on all my new releases. - www.Christina-McDonald.com/book-club

ABOUT THE AUTHOR

Christina McDonald is the USA Today bestselling author of What Lies In Darkness, These Still Black Waters, Do No Harm, Behind Every Lie, and The Night Olivia Fell, which has been optioned for television by a major Hollywood studio. Originally from Seattle, Washington, she now lives in London, England, with her husband, her two sons, and their dog, Tango. For more information, visit: www.Christina-McDonald.com

Printed in Great Britain
by Amazon

46009348R00091